Add your Book Title

Add your Author Name

Published in 2014 by FeedARead.com Publishing

First Edition

A CIP catalogue record for this title is available from the British
Library.

BENSON BENJAMIN SINGH BHAMRA

BENJAMIN

My story begins as I was taking a journey home where I had been I did not know however I was being followed. Everything that had happened to me was in the events of two of my friend's deaths. The first was my father and the second was my best friend Shaun after a spiritual event in my home I began to show the signs of cracking up or going mad.

There are quite a few characters from the start but on this occasion I will not tell you about all of them. In this particular story the main character is Benjamin, of course that's the title too. I am trying to create a new character he is in about his forties and is very successful, with loads of money, tall and slim, and well looked after. Although threw his experiences he is a little bit crazy. In this book he meets his friends accidently as at this point he was living on his own. How did I come across this idea well the character came to me as I wrote as this is fiction?

INTRODUCTION

This gave me the scope to write everything and anything and as a lot of the story was written from the top of my mind there was no research as the ideas that I have written are all made up from my imagination.
I want this story to take you on a journey but through your mind I have tried to write about romantic places such as heaven, forests, and planets with new people. I want the reader to go on a journey through my words I want them to create and recreate Benjamins journey in your mind.

Preface

The first character I would like to tell you about is Shaun he dies and he is reincarnated and comes back as the second character the crazy cat which humors me for having a cat in my story. As you will read there is a seagull that comes into the story a kind of replacement for the cat towards the ending. Then there's David a guru I added him to the story to kind of get the reader to think of money and to slowly push the other characters aside as his name is a spiritual one. Although he only plays a short roll I wanted to bring a little light to my story as Benjamin would. As for Benjamin he's a really kind of confused but extremely intelligent and he is a loud person but clouded and wants answers for everything there are other characters in this story such as a seagull and a tramp. As the story starts off quite quickly I wanted it to have shocking ending as you will read. This story took me about a year to complete because it has its up's and downs. I needed to find a way for the book to balance so I created a lover for Benjamin and in that created a new planet where he could be but only through his mind.

Chapter 1
Through the mind

I waited at the bus stop for the bus it only took a few minutes before people started turning up I was getting paranoid; within a few minutes I was surrounded by people.
The thought of meeting my killers had sent a rush of adrenaline to my body I could hardly breathe. I was a high profile actor I was one of the best I was

not a coward but I had to call my friend for a conversation to calm me down. He was a copper and he was too busy to collect me which was what the conversation was about. As I put my mobile phone down the bus slowly pulled up, the journey was not going to be long, down through the high street down past the Kings Arms which was a pub, along Quarry
Way and just around the corner. I did not take the whole journey once the paranoia had worn off I got off half way and decided to walk it was easier breathing in the fresh air rather than trying to breathe on a stuffy old bus. I had started to reminisce It was dark I liked the night all the lights it reminded of a journey that I went on when I was a kid. I was walking with my mother she was an old fashioned lady, rich and stuck up I was only five at the time. My father was a soldier right up until he died he was always drinking and reasonably aggressive, He was tall like six foot so it seemed. The thoughts were there only for a second and they surpass nicely as I got into a walking pace. I got busy walking the journey home and I was counting the sign posts and my steps, to keep me awake and focused.

What I saw was that was the best part of the journey I had decided. That is when I realized that I came from an extremely rich family I do not know all the details, although only that my great great uncle went to Harvard in America that was the very best university at this time and he mixed and befriended the very best.
While I was walking and thinking about these things I saw the most beautiful girl, she had dark hair, slim in stature, she was carrying a hand bag and she was walking a dog. Form what I could see it was a British bull dog.
Her beauty was astounding I could not miss the opportunity the ask this girl out I shouted across the road to her she was definitely the most beautiful girl I had ever seen. I had only seen the back of her head, a bag and the back of her leather jacket at the first moment. It was her style that pulled me.
When I got home I walked into the hall way stepping over the mail on the floor. I took of my leather jacket and made my way up stairs to my bedroom got undressed got into bed and pulled
the duvet over me tightly.
That evening that is when it started, my whole body began to ache, I had the cold sweats, a fever.

I began to hear voices. I could not feel my feet or my hands I started to weep I thought I was going
blind. The weeping went on for around an hour. My head ached so much I

had to go to the fridge to get an ice pack, it did not help I threw the ice pack down I was beginning to get angry. That's when something else happened to me and it started with a conversation, I was in a mess I felt hot all over I opened the windows in the bedroom to let in some fresh air.

I knew I could only help myself from the very beginning. I did not tell this to many people this but I was a drunk an alcoholic, the voices keep on mentioning it old thoughts they were all acting like they knew something they said so much in so little time. Just after this they said they were leaving but they took off their shoes and stood by the door it had started raining and I could not imagine them walking out into the pouring rain. There had to be a theory to this unsolved phenomenon. I could only imagine that they were not from this planet.

I closed my eyes and went into myself and asked my soul to follow
and that is when things got complicated I had not yet figured it out what I was going too.

I was told while I travelled in my soul that the person whom was doing the talking was me in the the future pretty grim I think. He was or should I say I was a messenger this was going to happen ten years from now. But again I was not sure. If that Was that really me.

At first I thought it was god the way he spoke, the way I had dressed I was in all white attire. Looking on the religious side of things I could have been an angel, sateen, an angel of death, god, the holy ghost, or even Jesus Christ oh yes and not forgetting aliens.

I came out of my mind I received a message I had to look at the term player what did this mean I know it means whatever it is it knows everything about everything and what the term everything is.

The voices in the back ground became extremely polite there was a voice that which I truly fell in love with. If this was the voice of god I was truly in the right place.

Once I had established what I was experiencing. Everything even the beat of my heart came to peace. Once I had written this down the voices departed. I went downstairs it was early morning by the time I had finished. I was walking down my stairs in the corridor when there was a knock my door. I opened the door keeping my face partially hidden and my feet were braced against it was the postman. He dropped the letter of closed the gate and walked down the street. I was going to throw the letter on the floor but somehow I managed to hold on to it. It was in a medium sized envelope, white in stature and it felt like it was worth something I hesitated to open it.

I went back upstairs got onto my bed it was large bigger that a two sleeper I liked my space. Especially in bed there are something that you can enjoy sharing your sleep time.

I sat back and closed my eyes it took me a few minutes to settle that's when I was at my most powerful then it happened I began to travel through my eyes into my mind there was somebody there they had not given up their identity there were two of them I could see both of them standing there they were both male the first male said to my surprise did I get the letter then he said I know you have it in front of you the second character just stood there. There was an amazing flush of color steaming through my soul red and greens purple and orange. I asked them a question what do they want, there was a large splutter a cough and them another sputter then finally he started to tell me. He began with opening the letter I could not believe it, a letter from the president so he was one of the figures in my mind that whom I was talking with it stated in the letter that the other figure could not be mentioned due to spiritual reasons but I have reason to believe that it that he was called the 25th one of 25. We spoke for hours discussing all kinds of things where the planets money was going and was it going to the right people other people with the same ability s as ourselves

was it god we were speaking through and how we had to keep our thoughts pure so we were safe from sateen and angels. I had to repeat some of the things to myself just to take them in.

I could feel the heat I asked him what that was he said it was fire it was a fire of coldness I had the lack of concentration which was leading me to sweat cold. I looked up there was a coffee drink in front of me it was large in a white kind of triangular shaped mug. That's when the vision had finished I opened my eyes.

That's when I met my other me

I came across as very polite that's when it was revealed to me that I was going to meet a princess which one I said gratefully she was going to take you into her eyes. I was told quite a few things about her but before my other self-left I did not give myself the name of this princess. I kind of made it up what the experience should be called it needed a title in the end everything needs a title I came up with real life cross dream experience I could feel her power from here she was in love with me. As I recall the princess was dressed in white but from a distant as she approached my mind her garments changed into a flurry of colors. The feeling was unreal I found it hard to except at first but the thought was so powerful I had no choice but to bow down to it.

I could look into her eyes, she was perfect, she had dark hair perfectly combed. I could not take my mind of her eyes they looked so pure that's when I feel in I was going to ask her for her hand she already knew this feeling of being there with her was like nothing I could imagine. The vision slowly past I fell into sadness then that's when she spoke to me it was sweet to hear her voice. I come from the planet on the right. That was cool and dangerous.

CHAPTER 2 THIRD VISION

That was enough for me for now that was the third vision of the day although by the end of the evening I was back in my room I had spent about three days and this was me forth night that I had
meditated myself across the other side of the planets and it was addictive. I gathered my thoughts again, I placed myself down on my bed and closed my eyes. I was moving fast in my mind for a few minutes that's when the journey I was taking stopped. I looked around myself nothing but sand, at the first instants I thought I was in Africa, the sun it was out and it was extremely hot I looked around up and down then into the distant I was on the edge of a desert. that's when I saw a kangaroo I was in Australia. I was hesitant to take a step forwards to see if the ground was hard enough to take me, as I did looking out into the distant I saw a figure it was walking towards me. When he got close enough he stopped and put his hand upon my shoulder. He said nothing at first and I was quick to question him.

I was meeting another president he did not seem to bothered that I was there and asked me why I had summons him to this desert which was his. After a great pause he spoke he said that there was going to be a great war he said that his country had become corrupt and that the people within a few years will turn against each other and that there were many things wrong and he wanted more help from me to correct this how could I help he said I was to take up the power.

There was already wars in the middle east he said that he would meet me in Africa he kept on mentioning the wars of the past and he also said that there was to many corrupt men in power and there will be another time when their own mind will destroy themselves in the background I could hear sirens and the sound of the wind began to get have disturbed me and I had to bring myself back.

I looked out of the the window from my bed the police had parked up outside it seemed very quiet or maybe it was just me. The thought of the police car outside was preying on my brain as if I was not disturbed enough, this time I got out of my bed I was still tired I closed my eyes the police car had gone and I smiled and went back to sleep but it was not long before something went wrong some someone had tried to contact me while I was asleep this was forbidden, it was a rule according to the letter which was the sent. I had the letter under my pillow where it was safe.

I had fallen into a deeper sleep in this particular dream, and a dream is different to a vision I do not know much about dreams or visions really but in this was new I looked up and to my surprise I was surrounded by people on one side of me was a panel there was for people next to each other and they were seated on different levels they were smartly dressed and they were talking amongst themselves. On the left of me was a girl she was small she wore or should I say she was dressed to smartly to except, she also wore a cloak it was large and looked heavy and on the other side was a tramp holding a sign with his name on it. It said homeless and hungry and had his name on it in big letters, I could not make out what he was all about then she spoke. He believes that he was the god of war, quoting that he was a poor fellow that welded a bus pass and could not afford his travel but where was this all relevant. It was not, it was just part of the game something to determine that the devil was real and he was still amongst some of us, she went on what if he had a job.

What was I supposed to do, I looked cross at the old man he began to look more and more familiar he was handing under this beard

It seemed that I had been there before except this place was becoming more and more unfamiliar and the people in it were becoming more and more unsettled. The girl refused to stop questioning the old man which supposedly was supposed to be me into leaving eventually the girl gave in the old man became powerful a sparkle of light came from his body and he disappeared. He had died. I fell to the floor it was painful watching yourself die. That was it I had seen enough. Had enough have you she replied I waited I was still on the floor when she said it, she was convinced that she had destroyed us both when I awoke I was sweating I knew that one day I am going to meet my maker if it be an old man or a little girl I had a rival this was quite common apparently in the realms of meditation. What I saw was a dream so nothing really happened but there was a possible chance that when I get old ill properly become a victim of hell like every person.

It was time to find myself as teacher, but first I had to bring myself back that's when I opened my eyes I came back slowly.

I jumped up and looked in the mirror my face had changed I had aged about ten years that's when I realized what was happening why did I not notice it before I went to my bedroom and opened the letter that the president had sent me while you meditate instead of growing younger you will grow older each time you use your mind in this way this letter is a warning and an invitation to join us do not be discouraged this letter also has the rules you will grow young again but only in time.

It was time for me to make more time for myself the whole situation of growing old before you grow young was beginning to get to me I did not take me long to figure out that I had been leaving myself

for dead while meditating in fact the thought was so strong I became light headed for a whole hour or two and worried with the thought. This continuous light headedness had happened before I remember the girl I meet while walking home I felt so bad because she did not answer me I just felt like dying this was the fifteenth time I had felt drowsy now after the meditation, I was counting and I wanted to rested my head on the toilet bowl a few minutes later I was sick the smell of puke filled the bowl and the taste was in my mouth I wanted to get up but I could not the only thing I could do was put my fingers down my throat an puke up again just to get rid of the feeling.

After this experience I knew that travelling through my mind could be seriously dangerous as for me things
we're looking a little bit dark maybe it's a start of a new journey which is supposed to be light.
I walked out of my house the wind was blowing in my hair I pulled my scarf around my face I had not been in the fresh air for

CHAPTER 3 ONE MONTH

outside for around a month consistent meditation I could feel my soul sucking the darkness into my mind. I thought to myself I have been to pretty fantastic places. I had not eaten for a month or drank anything I did not realize how thirsty I had become. I was in such a good mood I decided to walk the shopping Centre. I had eaten everything in the house the cupboards were empty. I liked to keep a low profile the first thing that I went for when I got there was some booze that was not so pure so. I'll try anything once just like everybody else I looked around the shop floor I found all the food that I wanted.

had got some shopping good s and payed at the till, the lady was quite nice nobody said a thing but it was like everybody knew. I walked home, sun slowly disappeared behind some clouds I was left with just the cold air.

The next thing that was going to happen to me was that I was going to meet her boyfriend I went into deep meditation as soon as I got home, I was trailing the journey I knew it's every turn how long the roads were. When the next turn was going to be. Past the Japanese restaurant. That's when I saw her the chick with the leather jacket and hand bag the guy whom was sitting next to me must have been a dreamer he did not even notice her. Hold on driver I said I want to get off. I jumped off at the next turning. What a gift I bumped straight into her, she dropped her bag I apologized and helped her pick her things up. I'm really sorry I said. She did not speak English but she bowed a couple of times to say thank you. She was shy I called out what's your name but I seemed to scare her off. I opened my eyes and brought myself back again. I stepped outside for some fresh air.

It was late when I got in I could not believe I was walking around half dead and beat I was not used to it. I was outside for a few hours. The wind got heavy I could feel hitting my face and blowing my scarf around. I bowed my head to stop the wind blowing too hard on to my face. when I walked it was like I was really fighting the elements each pace a dangerous step. When I got in my home I was greeted.

with load cheers and welcomes, welcome home the voices said I went straight to the toilet. I can't explain the feeling but it was like the room was sucking the light out of the side s of my face the first thing to do is throw up the feeling was that bad and dizzy I was not sick as such I was just over excited I think but this was not good not again. I asked myself when there was quiet I guess the voices were just excited to see me as I was them, they often said they missed me they were friendly but there was a feeling for this. I was just going to sit down when the worst pain I could imagine hit me. I knew that I was going to feel something I had the same weird feeling that something was going to happen all day long. I picked up the phone struggling to see the numbers on the dial. I had blurred vision it was not good.

I rang the local doctors there is as no answer I threw myself on to my knees and closed my eyes and prayed to god. I had tooth ache it was bloody painful and cold sweats, by the time I found a doctor I could not be seen. They were deadly serious about their business I had not realized but I had missed two appointments so they stuck me off apparently. I'll find another good doctor I told myself. The pain was not receding and I was desperate and in pain, I got lucky.

I found one on the edge of town. I left my home to go outside. The bright lights hit my eyes that's when I realized that I needed something they were simply a brand small, and came in many brands I wanted a pair of sun glasses I wanted to know if they could exist in my new world I do not know what to call it so I just call it the system. What I did not tell you that before I meditate I have to strip naked it is the way.

I found a pair most expensive plastic sun glasses they were dark and made me feel like a real star I walked straight in to the waiting room to the left of me was a toothbrush cabinet with toothbrushes and in it was some tooth paste, the room was full of people I tried to look intelligent as I sat down waiting.

and all the posters were scattered across the wall it was like a teenager's bedroom, it had been at least ten years since I had had a tooth ache I did not like the feeling but does anyone.

I could not wait any longer the pain was now unbearable I closed my eyes what's the answer I said it was like I was on a train the flashbacks mixed with dreams of paracetamol to ease the pain.

I kind of thought that it was the same with everybody. It was kind of paranoia. I was quite surprised with the turn out in the dentist. I had been waiting for about fifth teen minutes that is when I had the idea of jumping the que. There was an old man sitting right next to me I needed to know his name so I made polite conversation with him and at the end of the conversation I asked him his name shook his hand as this happened his name was called out I stood up slowly waving the old man back down on to his seat as I took his place to go in to the surgery room. As we started the removal of my tooth I began to realize that We did not get along in fact we hated each other even if I was polite she made sure that she hated me in the chair she made it clear. She did not know me it was just her way I always thought of myself now as a star, it was not something I did but it was said that I had changed the shape of the inside of my mind by meditation but I think it was stupid, irresponsible and a childish thing to do. So The power of meditation had begun to change the shape of my mind. I had to believe it I had seen everything that there was to see in the mind without actually going anywhere. Indeed, this was quite serious matter It was better than a science lesson. I had seen everything that there was to see and I had been everything that I was going to be. I looked out of my window it gave myself a piece of my mind.

I walked into the front room everybody was there the old man from the trail who was a tramp. the girl, the girl that was grilling the old tramp who I think was me was now having a word with the president and the 25th. It was a great debate. I closed my eyes for a second then in that instance I knew that I was in the wrong place at the wrong time. It was Just seconds before I was going to start making my way out of the place I blacked out through tiredness.

When I awoke I found myself tucked up in bed although. I was acting if nothing had happened as I was trying to hide the truth. I asked myself a question why was I here I asked. Don't worry they said you will be all right. I did not know where I was or whom I was speaking with. The only thought was of the girl there was an image that I could not get out of my head.

whoever she was she was caring for me I know, I looked around, in front of me was a mirror I struggled to sit up to it, when I did I smiled I could see clearly I was in the right hands, there was lip stick marks on my face and about my lips. I wondered who she was then she walked in it was her the princess. The princess explained what I could not believe, it was if they had brain washed my mind.

After this I could not think about anything else apart from the princess which whom I was in love with and still do and always will.

When I had meditated myself back to myself and got home. David the tramp was in my kitchen turning out my cupboard looking for something to eat.

take it easy said I reached out to touch him on the shoulder, that's when he spoke in one word he told me everything. I needed to know about everything in one thought the vision that he sent me raced through my mind at millions of miles per hour it was like riding a slip steam building over and over building the pictures in my mind until it was full.

I fell to the floor I was exhausted, when I got up he was gone and so was the food. I was about to crack up for some reason I kept on having accidents I took my jacket off it was ripped and looked dirty and went upstairs what' s the reason that I am being treated so badly. I had to ask myself if I had done anything wrong, then it came to me that the voices they have not been in touch which was problem a good enough reason to think that they were the reasons that I was in so much pain taken in to consideration that I never said to them that they had to leave so where were they.

One thing that I know if the media got hold of my stories what would they think. What would they write, well the night was young I had not felt like this for a long time but then I had a few bad nights it was not that bad. The fact that my dreams were scaring me is that why I woke up crying it was like I was a little baby waiting for my mummy to come and wake me and pick me up but that was not going to happen. Then there was good therapy but that was wearing off. I had to find to something to impress myself this experience was coming to the end and the whole system was on the brink of destruction. After years of meditation and preys and enlightening visions at least I knew that there was no other person but God that I would like to talk too.

The little people had become my new subject and my main concern I would sit there for weeks on end day after day just waiting to hear from them.
That night I lay there upon my bed in the same room I was a little reluctant to close my eyes I was frightened of what I thought of what I was going to see.
It's funny because if I told you that my best friend was in the same room as me watching me, watching over me.

I would be telling him to turn down the music or turn on the radio it was enough to drive you nuts. I closed my eyes and took of my clothes and put the sun glasses on and sat crossed legged on the floor I closed my eyes and it had begun I found myself in the same room as my cat the one that died I was sitting there on the floor I could feel this kind of silky feeling then it just walked out, it was my cat. I don't believe it who told you. I asked it not expecting an answer it replied everybody knows. even the

Chapter 3 one month

ground that you sit upon. At this point I Knew the cat was in on it, he could speak human.

"True". It said even though they hate you I'll be honest it does not mean a thing.
In fact, they do not care. Which in my eyes is disobedient?
The cat walked in as slowly as a panda his speech was somewhat different now he was a clever cat he shut the door after him I had no choice but to shout out to it my words were that I could meditate myself through that.

meaning the door.

Three months past I had meet the cat on numerous occasions he spoke of great riches and worldly things to be won in the spiritual world he often boasted that he had nine lives'. I always said it was a gift to be a human for me or anybody in a matter of fact.

A few more week past but the cat's visits had become less and less than the cat stopped appearing. I wondered where he had gone. I was so silly I did not think. It was not until I got another white envelope letter from the president that I found out that the

the cat had slowly past away again and was going to be replaced.

Replaced I said to myself replaced with whom. I did not take the subject up again it was too personal I remembered the cat it would sit on my bed without saying a word. The cat was a smart creative creature he will be dearly missed.

when I began to write I was busy writing my third novel it was big bigger than the first two I wrote that I had done as I had thought about his thoughts. As this is my cat and was going to meet him on the spiritual plane I felt excited. He returned but something awful had happened he returned but he returned as a killer he killed somebody and was sent straight to hell.

I saw him briefly before this terrible incident had happened I did not ask any personal questions as I remember he just walked in without saying a word and laid on my bed. He did not speak which was unusual He seemed different subdued the look on his face was not normal. His whiskers were wet and he could not stop licking his paws. I took a closer look at him his fur it looked rugged and hard not soft and shiny. the dirty deed was done he did not know anything more about it I asked him to meditate with me as he did before but he refused. There was a look of glee in his eyes that's when I forced myself to throw him off the bed and put him outside. He wondered in again and again this happened at least three times in away.

It was going to be one of those days I just knew I was told by a phone message that I was going to be baby sitting at exactly five O clock. I looked at the clock that's great I said to myself I had time to quickly get dressed as you do, jeans, t shirt, smart shoes what's the time five thirty or there about go just got time to catch the sun set I could watch that sky line all day. I might see a flying saucer or a space ship, all try and see if I can spot the number on a plane will be the little alien on the wing I'm just going to get my binoculars I said to myself the weathers good and the sky looks good too I was trying to be protective It was not as if was trying to protect the neighbors with this impassive attitude watching the sky's lights dim the winter nights and early afternoons.

I was wrapped up fairly warm but still felt the cold a part from my jeans which were torn in the knees and I had a t shirt and a jumper which I had forgot to mention. My hands were leading of the cold weather its always my too hands that's a fact. a star appeared I got all excited.

To me it was way up there I could point to it and just about make it out that's unreal. most of stars were good this one was not an evil star like the cat but it was right above my head it was a glowing, friendly, mature, a baby, I tried my very hardest not to notice but I could not help myself I had to say hello.

And that was that. It was said that if you disturb one star you disturb them all and that's a lot of stars to be disturbing you but I found that they were happy to be friend me they were happy that I was in control of them. After finding out this knowledge I was tempted to go public my attitude was like a spoilt brat and I knew this and I was always trying to change the way I was thinking.

I might get a response in the end. I went back inside I had just baby sat the stars and I had really enjoyed it.

Then in an instant after the experience that I had three further premonitions and two days later I had a virus I passed out again and ended up in the princesses arms she was always happy to see me and I was happy waking up to her. The princess handed me a mirror and asked me to look into it.

I looked in the mirror and pulled an ugly face I did it a bit more until I began to upset myself and smiled the princess. The princess then asked me what I could see. I waited for a moment I said to her that I did not need the mirror to see, she said in a very soft voice just look so I did. I saw myself throwing myself straight on to my knees and asking god for forgiveness. I tried to figure out that why was I throwing myself down on my knees and would I actually possibly do it. The princess asked me to practice it. so I practiced it for a minute or two I was a man of my word and of the lord I said she replied wise words.

Anyway this great experience I had become one with myself although now my body was aged.
considerable. I was wondering how I was going to turn my myself into the young man again. I went into

the kitchen and put some water into a kettle and turned it on. I was making a cup of tea. I had made it and I slowly sipped from the cup I was thinking
What annoyed me the most was it the cat or was it that I was living in town but it was just too noisy in the town as it was in the country side too I do not only know this through my experiences and they thought the same.
I picked up the cup of tea I took one sip of it and poured the rest of it down back into the pot. I then realized that was a waste and I said it to myself. It had begun to rain I could hear the droplets outside splashing on to the window pane and on the roof that's when the weirdest thing happened to me the clouds departed quickly like there was another storm was brewing it was like a storm on top of a storm the clouds were moving quickly. I looked up and sat down in a puddle the water it was ice cold, I planted my arms and hands down into the grass as I was on the grass. I closed my eyes what did it say I cannot remember exactly it was a whisper it was something like alpha aphelia the sky's had spoken to me for the first time I had find out what this meant.

It was the week end and the football was on I had put my life
aside just to listen to the game I like the football they always seemed up set the commentators I thought maybe it was me, the teams were quite excellent and exciting this is what I thought I liked most players.

The rebuilding of my mind and body was important to me I was not getting any younger yet that was the way most people end up. The music was another thing. I heard this voice it was loud it was spiritual I'm not sick I said I'm not a schizophrenic there was a second person too, but you hear things from time to time. Like you
understand. I knew who it was the voices they had finally came back, I turned up the TV
 back to watching the football I could not comprehend what I was about to go through

come on boy you know the routine drop them pants they were joking there was about twenty minutes to go but the voices were persistent they had par pared themselves I could tell. I was sitting there semi naked on the floor anyway I turned on the TV and sat down cross legged my arms aside of me my hands face looking down on the floor. My eyes became heavy in a desperate attempt to turn off the TV but it was too late the voices began their synchronized attack the sensation left me sitting up right it sent my body in to an over whelming fit of love the whole vision leaped me on to the TV. I could see everything but it did not stop there the voices had entered the program too. And they were being spoken about this it made me angry the colors in my mind began to change from black to yellow then too green and orange I was travelling faster than the speed of light. Where I was going I could not tell you at this moment I was surfing.

CHAPTER 4 In to the mind

All I could here was music the voices had entered the radio all I heard was can you hear the music can you hear that. when I landed I briskly ran my hands over my body there was a lady she was on the TV. It was a film that I was watching, there was a new feeling in my body, it was the first time I had mediated with the TV on it was dangerous even more so the radio was on in the
background. I was in ecstasy, all I know is that I was fond of her, it was not that teenage crush. And I was not the shy type but I was still a virgin and quite inexperienced. It was not just the film stars now it was the radio stars as well that's when the doorbell rang I struggled to my feet bringing myself back and hurried to the main door clumsily knocking over a vase on to the floor from off its table.
Express delivery a voice called out from behind the door. The mail it was a white envelope. What is the time I asked myself I looked down at my watch 3pm exactly it was the president I bet? I staggered on my feet and walked back to my room I was right. What was the warning.
this time I took the envelope and opened it up in large bright letters I said turn off the TV and turn the music off. I had no choice but to take his advice. I was a sucker for perfection in a specific way. I had been taught through my soul. It was sex, sex, drugs, and more sex. oh yes and who was getting richer and richer I was every day I have thought about it you no playing this

relationship was the most genius thing, what a wonderful thing to my soul. The voices had stop all I could do is sit there exhausted again.

The doorbell rang I could not be bothered to answer it so I shouted out I am not in. The doorbell rang again go away I said calmly it rang once more I forced myself to my knees the sweat poured of

my body Jesus it was my mum hi I greeted her doing that meditation again. I said nothing
all I could focus on was my mum I had to get her outside the house. She said I looked a state I agreed. I grabbed a towel from the bathroom. And walked her to the kitchen. It was not a long visit and a few hours later she left. I chose to sleep the rest of the day.

The next morning "hello darling she said haply what are you doing here I let myself in I thought there was nobody in."
"I see just having a snoop ".
"oh no do you think".
"I just came around to make sure you are all nice and tidy" she said that in a shimmering but sensitive kind of thought

Then there was another voice "hello"
"who's there" I called.
It's you knew house mate do you know the date.
You must be Eugene that s right she said with a smile and sticking out her hand I shook it she did not notice the sweat she never caught on.
But I knew somehow that she knew what I had been doing then she noticed your sweating she said
but before I had a chance to explain mother butted in

he is a mediator.
Sweat she replied "that's good"
that's when it happened I began to sweat cold oh no I said again.
Five minutes into the conversation she noticed
are you all right your sweating err she said trying not to notice it she them wiped her hand down her

blouse.

You are sweating profusely are you all right

I am yes I sweat a lot sometimes.

You should go lay down. Do you have a temperature?

I do yes

"The football dam it what the score". I had forgotten the football was on which gave me an excuse to quickly change the subject from how sweaty I was to the football results.

"2-0 I think."

"who scored".

"it was that foreign player".

they begin to laugh.

"what s up".

"it's your face you look well funny".

"just tell me the score".

"look we have done it"

they laugh again." that's it gets out that's enough ".

"your throwing me out wait a minute this is my house you have only just got here".

The music was blearing out but I was not really listening to it. All I could hear was my house mate taking about me above the music to herself. I wanted to think that they knew who they were that's when the oddest thing I thought that my mother went home

I went to the window and made sure it was shut. At least I knew who I was a fashion star, role model and movie star.

Going back to the football arsenal came back from being 2 goals down. I did not disturb my new house mate again I looked out of the window it was night time I have to admit she had quite a presents I kind of felt safe around her I looked at her resume model and role model it looked pretty good. The next morning, I went to the window I looked out   of the window their she was undressing in the garden first her top then her t -shirt. I turned away I had to be crazy not to peak.

I thought for a moment that I was a really lucky guy. It was me again I'm sure I was being drawn in some kind of super power I do not mean to turn the radio or the TV. It was a luxury for me to have music on. I wanted to know what kind of adventure she had in mind. She dived into the pool.

The day went past quickly there I looked out the window the love was still there she was sitting in the garden. Eugene was sitting singing. That is when I stumbled across the idea to put a film

on. the film I chose was a romance film do you think she would catch on was. I wanted to pull her. The movie that I put

was an epic adventure and romance movie I pushed the pause button.

Eugene was still sat there in the garden she was still singing it sounded good then the style changed rapidly to a rap song I will not go any further that. I sat back on the sofa put my arms on my head you could clearly see what was going to happen I was going to fall in love with her.

She came in and sat down next to me she never said a word but I was desperate to break the silence.

The conversation I wanted to start left my mind. I got up a went outside to practice what I was going to say to her quickly. she shouted out a few seconds later to see if I was OK. I then reversed the question are you, I shouted back.

Okay I silently said to myself the window cleaner had turn up. I wanted to know wanted to know the ins and outs of this chick you know what makes her click. Then I realized that it could be easier than I first thought I could meditate myself in to her universe. About fifteen minutes later she had walked in and sat down in front of the film. I had gone to my room. I am going.

ask the man at the top I said quietly to myself. She sat there watching the film I could hear her playing it from my room.

Things were getting more tense then the sweats began I had my answer from the top of my head.

I sat down I was semi naked I put the sun glasses on, she was not an easy person to find.

Eventually she gave in I got into her mind I could see her clearly she was golden she liked money

she considered herself a movie star, a film prodigy and an actor and play write. She said when I asked her what she liked to be called she said mogul. She was also well trained she was a sixth Dan karate and artist. She was everything.

except she did not have the big mansion the fast cars what she did have was
a good home and lots friends which I understood.
 I slowly went in looking for her friends I had found them, the first was this
guy called Richard they met at a bar in Soho. He was fit and young I meant
that in a good way. He was tall in stature there
was a dark side to him he said that his brother had committed suicide

I could feel her power she as strong it was scary but she was so pure in her
heart. Trying to find a way out of her was going to take me to
the edge.

by the time I had finish it was 4. oo pm she was on the phone
I know mum but he understands me the conversation went on me, why, what.
His stature no he does not look like a gorilla, no he has not got a belly either
yes of course he's had a drop before.
About 6 ft. and holy the conversation ended with that.

What was going to happen to me I said I properly go to hell for all my sins.
I just hoped that she would make to the same heaven as me. We met in the
hallway we practically bumped into each other that s when we hit it off. We
stood there talking for hours. We were coming
to the end of the conversation the last questions she said after great debates
we discussed how many heavens there where she said none I said seven I did
not want to discuss the subject any more so I said I want to take a break, my
jaw was aching from all the taking. But she went on for hours more, I was
impressed but unsure that I should answer her questions the answer to these
questions would only upset me. In the end she said she loved me and Jesus
Christ. Well that took all day I said to myself and briskly walked to my
bedroom

The next Morning, I woke up I was still feeling tied I tried to get back to
sleep I tossed turned and fell out of my bed. That's when I asked myself
another unorthodox question what was sleep
and where did it come from. Why do we need more as we get older and
where does the conscious come from and how the soul knows and control? I
know what I was doing was travelling through my conscious going to place
to place.

I had many visions and dreams, they take me way back to the days when I had travelled across to the America I must had been there sometime in my last life. somehow we are spiritually connected.

The dreams I had were getting worse and harder and harder to understand I was thinking a lot of people would disagree that the dreams and visions I am having are true I am not knowing the

exact truth about what I see and hear.

All I can say whatever it is it is well hidden inside of you. It was when I had awoken I had soon realized what had done. My first thought was to wash and clean myself up. The second thought was I wished I had a dream well I hoped for God's sake it was a dream but it was not it was very real. I was dreaming about a dream as an I sat in the chair the thoughts were streaming into the point that I had blocked my own mind stopping the thoughts and images I wanted to learn how to act. I wanted to be an actor, the thought was overwhelming. It was taking me to new kinds of places. My thoughts wondered around and around all day long that's when Eugene walked in.

I could smell booze I smiled your drunk but then the tears came to my eyes.

I felt my flesh crawl for the second time the first was this morning that's when it all came flooding back my memory was on fire, picture after picture I sat there watching her well into afternoon so what is your style

there's no style to it just be yourself if your gay it helps if you are a little bit Kamp

I can do Kamp

relax breathe

the lesson went on for hours we were having such a good laugh I was like it was meant to be there was a connection between us we were defiantly meant for each other. We both ended up on the floor I had her in my arms.

Later on the two other house mates were about to arrive I left the door open so they could just walk

in there was a loud hello I replied with a shout come through.

Nice to see you

your welcome

so what have you been doing

not a lot she said

come on I'll show you around I showed them the whole mansion then I took both of the them down

stairs to the games room. The games room was my personal space I made it quite clear that it was a no go area and to get in you needed an invite from me. It was only for computer players. I had the latest games consoles and about 1010 games nobody had a collection like me. I could use a computer fully by the time I was 11 yr. s old. I had hacked into several banks and made them offer me money, by the time I was 16 I was imprisoned in a youth policy treatment Centre I also had a brutally knackered nervous system the computer ate me and my nerves and that was my greatest achievement. I continued.

nobody, I was half way through a conversation that would be a great achievement I was saying but I reckon that not only would he open the front door but he would answer the back door as well and on top of this he would do the cooking and the cleaning to. I was just complimenting my two new house mates they were so polite and tidy I had to remember my manners.

I had actually had enough for one day Dave was OK so was the guru and so was Eugene. I wanted to know the ins and outs of the guru he had a spiritual name but how spiritual was he I said.

That was to come later first I had to get rid of my old memory. So I told the lord to unload my old

memory it was an amazing feeling my soul came out above me and touched my mind the whole front

of my forehead flicks it's self-up into the air I had lost my mind again there I had been unloaded now I asked the lord to save me just one more thing left to do is to close my eye s just for a minute to see what was in there.

A cigarette and a nice glass of wine to celebrate, I went down into my wine cellar and picked up a bottle of champagne. When I got back from the wine cellar I grabbed a couple of glasses from the kitchen and walked to the living room.

What s on TV I asked pulling up a chair and popping the bottle open it made Eugene jump the football was on? Who's playing.

Arsenal

what again.

The monsters were coming home I do not know why I said that maybe it was a child hood thing. Eugene wanted to talk about her child hood. The guru was there listening and advising her he was a good listener. The Guru just sat there we were all intrigued. I even began to feel a little sorry it was a sad tale for someone who had such a great influence in people I could see her destroying herself I had to stop her we were no longer strangers the doors of our pasts were going to be opened and our mind's interacted and closed.
The Guru was making us all smile so I sent him down to the wine cellar to fetch me another couple of bottles. had decided that we were getting drunk. It was easier to ease the pain when you were drunk and you can never remember what was said the next morning.

We sat and talked for hour each of us taking a turn I was good I felt like somebody again I got so drunk just wanted to talk about everything except on this occasion I left the meditation out of it
I really thought hard weather or not I should share the secrets.

I had to make the excuse of wanting to get another bottle from cellar to escape telling them the truth
that is when I got a message from the delivery boy. There was a knock at the door I staggered to the front door and opened it there was man standing there holding out his hand in it was a letter he thanked me and left. I opened it quickly and nervously said to myself "damn presidents going to war". It read after great consideration I have put many thoughts and after the long process of many talks and discussions we have come to the theory that we have no choice but to declare war on the world you are with me we want total destruction of the human race It was sighed I turned the letter over.

Well the spiritual world was going to war where will the players go if there's going to be a war.
It was a joke I'm sure the spirit was not as strong as the human body it can only sit and torment.
I think he's fighting a losing battle or he is going win one.

I waited for everybody to go to bed I stripped off and got on my bed I sat in my normal position and closed my eyes and waited and waited then suddenly with a second I was there it was it was true there was going to be war. I looked around there were body's everywhere children crying I took a child right up into my arms her tears escaladed down her face I asked what her name was she said Noah

what happened here I asked her she explained.

 I sat down by a rock closed my eyes I was going to find the president and 25th and see if we could find a suitable answer for the problem. I had sat there for about three days the guys in the house were getting concerned because I had been out of my room. It took me a few more days I was looking for a place to hide but everything was destroyed. The best that I could was to do was to hide in an ordinary old hut I was dragging the bodies in, bodies after bodies I moved from province to province. I was going into shock the bodies and the destruction and everything it was too much to take. They had ruined everything and if this was going to be in my mind I was going to be worried for a long time. In a way it was a lesson and I made a note that I would tell my children and they would tell there's and so on.

When my house mate knocked on my door I just had to tell them that I was busy and that they should go away

Eugene became forceful I had to convince her that I was alright and spoke to her through my bedroom door. I was using the time to find them the war torn victims.

Chapter 7 voices

Meanwhile Eugene was going on about something completely different I had bumped right into her mind, all I could see was the thought and it was a man, he said loved her well infect it was totally the opposite I could see that now I was in love with her. I had never raised my voice but I was slowly tempted. Who was this man were did he come from and why was he after my wife?

I have become everything you said that I would become and it is your fault. In fact, all I did was act and I think you made me feel real jealous but in fact I was not ready to perceive. I locked her inside of me she was extremely hard and I wished upon the hardness of her character which I had created in side of me would not die. Having been slightly side tracked only in hearing what had been said. I fear that I may have over visited her.

I was done for the day I got up got dressed and walked out of my mansion and went into town to the café when I got there was no nowhere to sit I had ordered my coffee and I was trying to put the morning' s thoughts behind me. I was standing up it was like being head boy. all over again everybody was welcoming me with open arms. I got a big hug from some bloke then there were cheers and singing people just going crazy. I have not been patted on the back so many times before. The cafe finally empty's about dinner time and I found a seat I looked on the menu and took a sip of the coffee. Just before I sat down I thought I was going to cry was everybody in the cafe actually was laughing I said to myself I must have missed the joke where they laughing at me. I asked myself. I could not express the feeling of my luck everything had slowed right down in my mind. It was like when you watch old people walk it was like it was in slow motion and the crazed man being falsely fed by a lunatic even worst it was like taken your medication, do it quickly I had to admit that the medication tastes like it had gone off even which a slow glass of water.

I coughed and swallowed deeply and then coughed some more I rubbed my chest. That is when knew.

the pain was so abrupt it was like taking a bullet or worse, although the pain was not in my mouth like a broken tooth but was like a swift pain straight to my heart I thought I would say that I have falsely fallen away from the girl that I had loved. I passed out.

The next evening, I had woken up sitting up right. The blanket that I was leaning on was not mine and the man that was sitting on it was not a friend I did not know the man who shared it with me. I looked around all I could see was the old man and a clear white ceiling as I was looking upwards. I asked him if the fruit that was in front of me was mine and if it was not if he would kindly remove it. The voice of the man seemed familiar.
I know you I said speak I want to hear your voice he spoke out after 5 or 6 minutes. I caught on it was the president I could not believe it I was saved. I actually started to laugh it had been the first time in ages. I laughed and laughed it was lucky if anything. That is when they walked in the man that was sitting there the president disappeared to my amazement.

It was going to take me all day to get my head around that I was left with a disgruntled look upon my face. With a new story in my mind I wanted to know where the man went.

It was Dave the guru and Eugene I could not recall her name I started with a stutter I could hardly move my mouth. A few hours later I could say one word it was Eugene.
Eugene smiled is that an old girlfriend she said it's me. She smiled again and said come over here lover boy and give me a kiss. I was just about alive when her name came to me
lips. As she kissed me the life streamed into my body. Time was ticking away I could not make eye contact due to the embarrassment of finding myself where I was. You passed out just looked at the clock on the wall. I knew I was in bed and that s about it, I did not know how I got here it took me a while to recognize who the people in front of me were. I asked them if they were my friends all the other people in the room were visitors. I closed my eye s and fell asleep. The next day in the morning I was greeted by Dave he handed me a cup of tea I spilt it over myself straight away I was that weak I could not hold the cup.
That's when the girl walked in I had forgotten how to speak she was not good looking and I was not going to desert my friends. She strolled over she was holding a paper in one hand I could hear her thoughts. That was not the thoughts of a meditator but the thoughts of a street drug user someone who takes mind altering drugs to change the shape of the mind so they could be like me I could see that she was in some kind of pain I know it' s a sad rule but we are taught to dispose of people like that for abusing their spirit. I tried to talk and it was so frustrating I attempted to shout in the process ripping my voice box apart the loudest I could speak now was more or less like a squeak.

I hummed for a while hoping that a word would pop out then this lady walked past Dave was sitting there just talking I was not realise that he was right next to me listening. I had more interest in the people coming and going.
She stopped right in front of me she was not very tall she was fat and slowly

spoken she said to me as she passed by my bed I had great respect for the poor they will die first.

Two second s later a girl walks in dressed in black. Dave the guru said I was to listen to him yeah I
said go on I'm there, I said coolly. I was still struggling to talk at this moment then some old woman started crying and shouting. Her father had just died, she picked up his jacket and removed his wallet and out it in her purse, Dave the guru saw it to he looked at me and asked me if it had meant anything to me I had not brought my wallet with me we smiled. Dave the guru was a quiet person he went over to comfort her and basically told her to shut he hell up he was not too remorseful she had got the money. I looked up the words slowly came to my mouth I could speak again the sentence which came to my mouth the words where you would not understand. I began to smile and I laughed I knew he would understand. The young girl that was hanging around the doormen try helped the old lady and started to comfort her again she was in tears but you could clearly see that she was a money grabber. Then I heard a voice it calmly said.

I vet got tortoise blood, I looked down I believe that there was a little boy boasting to me. He was dressed in a fancy dress costume he said his name was the turtle he was well spoken and

Chapter 10 out of the water

told me and Dave the guru that he could not express the way he was feeling although I could hear him swear and curse under his breath as he spoke I was always right it never came to my mind at the time just to shout.

Many people claimed that they knew me and wanted to experience the same as me when I walked outside they said I was walking with the sheep. Suddenly a load of people walked in. A lady in a pink top walk in she dropped her business card on to the table she was given them out to everybody. The lady lent on the dinner tray on one arm. I had never seen her before, she was slim but her head did not go with her body maybe it was her hair cut it was bundled up into a nest and her eyebrows were bushy and her clothes tight with a large chest. And to top it off her glasses were at the end of her nose. What the guru asked. Life insurance she replied. Dave the guru and myself just burst out laughing and sent her away. She was not impressed. It was late I wanted to go home in fact I was going to ask Dave whom had fallen asleep to get me some food there was nothing a good feed. It was a dream the last time I ate out was in the late 90s let the good time roll. Although it was hospital food but beggars cannot be choosers.

There was one time I was at a football do my best friends mum and husband all got drunk and even funnier my best friend sat down to eat and missed his seat. I've got some photographs somewhere. I finally got off my ass

things in the real world were getting too serious. I was told one day by a voice on a tape message that I was not to do any driving under any circumstances I had not driven since then for a couple of years and the rent that I brought in from the two lodgers gave me enough money to buy a car that is it, the freedom of the road. It was not long before I was on the road I enjoyed driving at night especially though did not go out often I was really ready for a drive. I put the keys into the ignition I was ready to go. I leant back in the racing bucket seat foot on the pedal. Then I stopped being laid back already I put my hands on my head. And that was it driving experience over and done with for the night. In fact, I had not gone anywhere I was too paranoid.

"Go far did you".

"about as far as the drive way".

"why did you buy a car your obviously not going to drive it."

"yes I will just give me time".

"you have had it for weeks." "you're better off riding an ox".

"maybe in India."

I was dreaming I could hear the police sirens in the background I did not know whether they were real or whether they were part of the dream.

I just wanted to finish the game the boss man told me that the keys had been locked in the car

for the first time I did not understand the dream there was no significant s.

I sat in the smokers hut the smell was quite distasteful the taste of my first cigarette for the day. The air was quite humid, I could hear the birds and the traffic surrounding me, the building on the left was a drop in Centre, the door that just slammed was the door to the entrance the smokers room. There patience's all came out one by one they all said hello I stood there silent I did not want to speak and I sure as hell was not going to start making friend's or start talking about my mental problems. I finished my smoke and walked across the hallway. I was about to meet some really crazy people again it had only been a second since I had met the first lot. In fact, today I will always say I made some of my best friends on that day. They were good people and clean

and polite they were just mixed up kind of like myself.

They gave me anything I wanted clothe s food, cigarettes and conversation.

There was a man there he was dressed in a black suit jacket he had short hair, scruffy jeans and shoes. His name well I was not sure now as we only met briefly. There was another man he came out side as I was walking in to the building he was dressed the similar jeans t-shirt and trainers.

I wanted to know if clothes made a difference in society. I had often been seen in a sweat shirt. I been wearing the style since I was a kid, they had never been in fashion. I had been wearing mine because it made me feel comfortable it was grey I loved it. By the time I had stopped dreaming

or thinking about what clothing signifies what things you might be up to in your life a girl called Cathy joined me I could tell that Cathy was going to be a friend Cathy was younger than me about 10yrs I enjoyed talking to her very much. Cathy always went on about being a football manager I hope she makes its. She was a smoker too and always offered me cigarette I always said no and just laughed it off. Then there was Sam, Sam was the boss she knew everything about everything

Sam was the top cat Sam could pull you in and push you out. Sam was very clever. what I a liked about her the most was her style she had a lot of money that's why Sam drove two cars she had a company car to a Volvo convertible and Tm2. People about her were always thinking of her money. We all wished we had that kind of riches. I like cars to I had expensive tastes the cars I loved were super vehicles. Dave guru walked in as I walked

out. I need a cigarette. Dave the guru's stature as I remembered it 6,2 tall with a long uncut finger nails classy teenage jeans, and a mountaineering jacket he was about 46-59 and he looked like wolverine out of the comic book

I had heard him talk he had a quiet voice.

Then there was nick he was a busy fellow always doing something he was straight never drank did not smoke and often but butted into conversations satire was up right a very stern kind of character. I do not know how he got here but somebody was out to screw him up I could tell. He had that look of concern on his face. As soon as spoke he got up and adjusted his seat he did not sit down again but stood there talking. Dave guru was busy with his healing stone's. On the other side of the room he said in a soft voice "you're going to be aright" it was not if he could tell that I had a hundred problems. Everything stating that I had a hundred more. Once I had told him this he got up and walked away I hoped he would come back. The birds were noisy and the roads were getting noise.

Two men came out and walked right up to me and started talking about holy things they had to be mediators but I could not be sure then the girl came out. My lips were sealed I wanted to listen to the two chaps then Dave came out again I was beginning to think that Dave was an old busy body.

we had an interesting conversation, now the men were now talking about music or something I was sitting down I was not looking at anything or anybody I looked up again the guys were talking to me I did not even know they were trying to quiz my brain. The next thing that happened to me was that I was going to meet the man in charge he seemed nice enough we did not question each other two much for every one question he asked me I asked him double. He was convinced that I was crazy

there was a meeting in the shed, the shed room was going be made an into a music room there was quite few musicians about me here too. I was convincing that I was in the right place. I had to tell the guys at home and Eugene I was ready to handle a relationship although I was warned about making too many friends it had happened before when I was a teenager. I seemed to draw people to me I do not understand the actual power.

Girls was the subject I was no pimp or even considered myself a good lover but I could not get over the fact that I fancy every girl that I see, weather it was on the bus, in the high set, or the weather girl on to, whether it was rich, poor or if it had a good job or walked or drove whatever it was I was in love. Eugene knew it so did Dave and the guru said I well I will not repeat it, I on the other hand. I just thought of it as being sophisticated who wanted to be tied down. I did not fancy my new friends even though friends hit on friends the women in the Centre were a lot older than me. Then I saw an old friend she saw me first she says it couldn't have been more confusing conversation everything I

Chapter 11 I was being stupid

said came out upside down in the end I got a slap in the face. I had to go home I left after saying good bye to everybody. I told them that I had to get back to do the gardening. The guru was the man he kept everything good the garden there was nothing wrong with the garden. Just before I left I got caught in an another conversation. I thought it was going to go on forever it was like a mothers meeting in here my mind thought. what's going on, I stared in amazement unable to speak and give an answer as the speaker was speaker was so fast. It's been a whole three minutes since you have closed your mouth I said I was watching a girl called Alison she shouted out and I am going to put this one out on you.
I left with the thought I did not understand her. Until she walked up to me and put her fag out on my jacket and just looked at me expecting a reaction but there was none. When I got home the paranoia hit me like a brick in the face. I tried talking to myself to make it go away. This was a feeling that I knew and it was not false to me. It was imposed on me by another man that I had met some time ago. if I remember he was an old house mate.

In the end the truth will come out whether I live or die I had not planned on dying yet exactly while I was still discussing my child hood with Cathy Ann and my consciousness or what was left of it as it had been ripped out of my brain. I looked down at the table I only did this when I did not want people to notice me I looked down at the pen also. Teaching and learning were the greatest gifts along with wisdom and love and peace. What was going to be my gift to mankind along with the gifts of speech we spoke about things which you could not maintain things like what was a thought, how many forms of communication' s was there how did languages come around and we discussed our own theory what is a normal thought if the thought is put in

front of you then yes and if it's what you see then yes and where do your thought s go after you use them how many thoughts you would use in a life time I know I was correct and there was nobody to challenge me .
I looked over my shoulder Cathy was there Ann was talking to Alison.

When I got home I felt exhausted something was not quite right I felt a lot of emotion. I thought about it for a while maybe too much the tears filled my eyes I began to realize that it was the right thing to do.
There was a scuffle and the sound of feet coming down the hall way I pick up a cup of coffee which was sitting on the side it cold and properly been sitting there for days. They both bundled in to my room hello then I knew that she was going to notice
"what's up".
there was a pause
"are you crying ".
"No of course not it's the coffee its hot", I put the cup up to my face to hide my tears again.
"Hi dude"
"hello guru"
It was Dave
 He walked into the kitchen half asleep he was supposed to be taking an early night.

"Group hug".
they both stepped up and put their arms around me. After five minutes they both cleared off shouting that it was good to have me back. I knew they were cool.
I was not bothered that I was drinking alcohol which I mistook for coffee all I was bothered about was covering my tears at that point in time.
    The worst thing about me was that I could see things that were not really there I felt like I was being haunted and haunted by the things I could see I could not explain. The voices that I could see were not
real either they would come and go, and all they did is piss me off I took another sip of the coffee which was whisky and spat it out instantly I had gone off the taste. A paranoid feeling came over me but this was a good paranoid feeling.

I looked up and scratched my head and the cook was just leaving I did not even know that I had a cook. He said good bye just as he was walking out he stopped. He was tall in stature short grey hair well-built body with skinny legs. He then began to question me because we had not met. In the end I finally convince him that I was his boss and he went home.

I was back in my house the voices were out amongst me and my mind they said that the sun will be out soon I replied "yes" but I thought for the first time why were they here by me, but it was all false the happy faces and the money. If these people really cared they would be up there but they were not, they were down here. In a way they were a compliment I was trying to look on the bright side of things but on the inside they were just like you and me ready to screw somebody over it was a well-kept secret until you knuckle down and wake up.
I walked into the lounge Dave was there on the phone it's your mum
"give me that" I snatched the phone from out of his hands. Which was out of character. He knew this and so did I. But he kind of just sighed away and I waved my hands franc ally to him sending him outside of the room. I was watching him as he slipped through the door. I then waved him back into the room.
there's a pause I handed the phone back covering the it so I could not be heard.
    "wait" I said. " tell her I'm out doing the shopping".
    "I heard that."
    "mum".
    she continued is everything alright.

The next journey was about to begin in time I was going to have some fun this time I was going to stand somehow it would make a difference I took off my jeans, pants, socks and t – shirt and put on the sun glasses this was new I knew that there was going to be a difference the sensation it was as if I was flying extremely fast rather than a floating driving feeling and I was able to see more it had widened my vision an extra 50%. I had entered a small room it was filled with old pitchers and paintings I had never been this far into or through my mind before. It reassembled a temple. On the other side of the

room was filled with writing's and books
and all types of messages from writings in the past.
When I finally stopped looking around the thing that caught my eye's the
most was the light it was pure black a lot darker than that I had ever
experienced and a lot darker than I was previously used too.
I had got the sense that I was outside the color had changed again as I looked
around. The light penetrated my back and went through down through my
body and up to my brain. I was thinking that I was in the wrong place for a
moment and I wanted to bring myself back. I was in an extremely large
garden on what seemed to be an estate. The garden was vast rows and rows
of trees. I wanted to walk back in so the light changed again I found myself
walking through the large corridors in the mansion, it did not take me long to
get used to the extremely large building That's when I found a vault. I was
thinking about what mum said to me on the phone but that kind of surpass as
I had found the vault. I grabbed the vault wheel and turned it span
uncontrollable until it stopped the vault was too hard for me to open it by
myself I was just about to give up when I heard a voice say "open it with
your mind".
I closed my eyes and used the thought it was done. I could hear my mum as
well. Mum always said you don't get something for nothing you get
something for something. Inside the vault was money I stood there for a
moment there must have been millions and millions in there it was
everywhere stacked high to the celling I was not going to touch it I was not a
theft that was not why I was making these journeys into my mind I wanted to
learn and explore I had enough money of mine own besides how would I
bring it back. I stood there for ages thinking how I could shift it.
I closed the vault and went back outside, it began to rain I could see the rain
drops falling on the floor and the sound of the pitter patter was getting louder
and louder, the voices were

busy discussing why I had not taken the   there was no point it was not going
anywhere and I knew I could find it at any time.
Chapter 12 pick it up

There was the subject of peace something that the human mind in the modern
world should try to accomplish maybe I could take the money and use it. I

went back into the mansion and entered the dining room. The meditation was for me was so addictive every time I made my way back I would feel sick you know cold sweats sleepless nights aching back I made my way back through my mind. I was busy now I had forgotten who I was all I could think about was winning my soul back. It was going to be a huge battle. I could imagine it could be like a war. On the way back I met the old man again Dave I was beginning to believe that he was not a real threat but I found him really annoying although

I kept on seeing him around me on a number of occasions I just did not want to mention him he was just beginning to get inside my head.

It was funny just a second ago I saw a friend he stopped me and asked me for a cigar he had questions. It was kind of like a mind check just to see if anybody experience the same as me. A few saints and a couple of priests, the whole of the church I do not know who else comes into mind. I began to see that somebody was going out of there way the better my mind. Well a point taken I am wanted was the thought I know now that I am a wanted man and I know when I am not wanted, and I know that I want in a different way. I am one.

Gary walked in and old friend hello I said greeting him. He was a care taker and was really friendly he was tall and worn he wore an old jumper the typical type of clothing that a hobo would wear blue trousers, suit jacket and grey jumper. I did not look up this time I looked down. Something suspicious was occurring around my thoughts what I looked forwards and down at his feet, my head was firmly in motion of facing down and in the background I could hear a cup of tea being made the echo of the spoon being stired around the cup echoed right into my brain. I could hear another friend walking in it was shaun and other members talking behind me, the radio was playing it was as if everything had been slowed down. Somebody slams a door. The conversation that had started was of discomfort. I on the other hand had been cursed from the very bones of my feet to my head. I was being pestered by a girl because I loved another. That's the reason why I was there, I had caused jealously and believed that my love for her was a curse. There were some children around me and the other members. I tried deeply to look happy. If they were children like myself I asked myself how would it be a curse, I asked myself again there was no answer and I thought about it hard. I had over spoken when a rush of thoughts reached my mouth and not my mind.

I was standing inside by a door now and I was in the way I tried to move into space but more and more members would walk in. Another and another and another then that's when I saw her. I had never seen anybody like it before. She had dark brown hair and her plain face reminded me of my mother. This was the second time I had meet like this it was a perfect look. I looked away so that she would not notice me when I looked up again she was making her way to the fire exit. That's when a shimmering light came over me it was most overwhelming then Gary walked by a gave me a nudge and a wink.

All the door of the building was open in the building and that's when I heard it I could not

believe it I could hear this squeaking voice I was too shy to answer it let alone understood it. It was something that I could not comprehend why me. After all the people who I stopped in the street and all the people that I had meet at this Centre I was still the only person who could see and hear. The things that only a crazy even person would see maybe I was crazy but could not see it. I shouted by mistake it just came out I wanted to know why. Was it something that I had done, or was it something that I had heard or was it something that I had read. Surly meditation could not cause these kind of symptoms. And if it did why was not I warned about this. The next stop was the bus stop it was still raining I was soaked right through I tried to dry myself off with my jacket, it worked for a little while. To walk was not that bad thing considering the weather I was got off the bus to walk home alone but it was only a short distance I did this on my own quite happily, I was quite paranoid at one part of the journey. On my way home I saw Gary on his bike he was racing it the roaring of the engine bike was ripping my ears apart but only for a few seconds. We were good friends but we kept silent. Sometimes silence is the best relationship. To be honest we hardly said a word to each other it was like we were telepaths or something. All we would do was look at each other and we would make each other laugh. Laughter was good I think we laughed for around Five minutes last time we spoke. We laughed over anything and everything. I was timing it on the clock the clock was on the wall in front of me in fact it when I looked at it I was sure that it was telling the right time but at the second glance it was wrong. I looked at my watch I was right it was wrong. That's when I realized that I was going to miss my bus when I got to the Centre. I knocked on the door.

I had just made it home and to my surprise everybody was out. I knew there was something wrong nobody had left me the key although I had already had one. But it was not for this lock. This had occurred more than once this was the third time this week.

It was getting cloudy outside; it began to rain I stood next to the back door. perched under the ledge of the back door hoping that the weather would not get any worse. The house that I was resting upon was an old restaurant it was converted to a six-bedroom Victorian mansion it had a huge garden. I remembered when I was young I would play here for hours outside in the sunshine but it was raining outside now if I could dance it would bring the sun out. The rain was slowing down slowly pouring out of the of the the over filled gutters onto the pateo flooring. I closed my eyes.

Shaun and I knew the girl she came out with all smiles again. The traffic in the background slowly became silent. Ann and Sarah walked towards me we were all by the bus stop. A bus pulled over Gary was next to it on his bike clumsy reversed his engine, Sarah busts out laughing she says to Ann that it was funny, another lady walked past the bus shelter She was old and looked worn she had her hands full of shopping bags we should have helped her. A few minutes later Sarah's bus turns up. It all went quiet that's when a loud voice shouted out that's my stop.

Your supposed to push the button when your bus stop comes near.

What button, what stop.

That was tough luck she had missed her stop and in saying that it the smile of her face slowly dropped into a sad look. The bus turned up and we all got on it. Ann did not say anything she just lit up another cigarette. We asked her to put it out as we were on public transport. She ignored the fact and continued to puff it even worse when she had finished she stubbed it out on the bus floor. Not that it meant anything but a pour attitude. She did not know at the time but you only get one chance in my book.

I was slowly hoping that the keys to my mansion would arrive, the Post man was supposed to bring to me this morning. It was a new mansion a little different to my other mansion in town. To be honest this was more like a winter retreat. I did not visit the mansion enough to call it home. I had put the keys into a parcel knowing that I was going to be here at the mansion in the morning ready to meet the postman. The rain slowly stopped but in a few minutes started again. All I wanted to do was get out of the cold and into the warm.

I questioned the question.

The roses in the garden looked good they were at full bloom there was lots of flowers in my garden I planted most of them myself, mind you in saying that there was one road cone, a skip, large pine tree, some benches to sit on. I could see all the way to the drop in Centre through my mind, and I could visualize the people, the parked cars, the inside of the old buildings which was a children's home beforehand everything, the fridge freezer, the cuboids, the celling, and floors everything the stairways and last of all the art the pitchers on the walls I could also see the blind, the dead and the dumb. I closed my eyes and brought myself back. Meditating outside seemed rather peaceful but not that exciting.

I was sitting in my bed room the doors and windows were closed and I think the bedroom door was locked I had some music on nothing special just an old cd.

I took a large mouth full of water out of a large glass which was sitting on the bedroom side board I could see the little droplets

Chapter 13 Actors never die

of water left over at the bottom of the glass. It must have been hot outside but as I recall in the visions it was always raining. I put the glass down wiped my mouth and slowly closed my eyes.

This was great I had never been to top of a mountain before and this mountain was the biggest that I could ever image I checked my ruck sack what I had in it. There was water, a blanket, a pair of shoes, a jacket, some food and a pair of gloves. it seemed so similar the paths like old trails something that I seemed to recognize. It was built into my mind kind of like a bird before it can fly it knows itself what its wings are for and it will throw itself out of its nest to achieve this so I believe that this journey is already mapped out in my brains so that I could see this vision. So up the mountain I walked I knew that I was walking in the right direction and before I knew it I was meeting other walkers, A young man caught my eyes. I knew him he seemed familiar I had never meet anybody with his statue and posture he was quite short he was still a boy. There was a girl as well I could just about see her she was right at the front. I could not reach her so I called out her but she never heard.

It was still raining it seemed to rain wherever I went. In fact, I checked the weather by mobile phone I was glad it worked and had not run out of power. They said there was going to be sunshine what I got was far from it. I looked down at my hands and thought that they looked weird. was something wrong with them I could feel something there was quite a lot wrong with me. When I looked at my hands I got the notion to think about the sides of

my head which I could not do without thinking about my eyes. I tried to think about my feet but that was impossible too. By the time that I had finished looking at my feet I decided to look at the rest of me

body I looked up, down, left and right. It was time for me to leave to the mountain. I said good bye to the other walkers and left. When I got back the next day I went straight to the drop in Centre. In the car park was Sarah, an, and Gary. It was late around 12 o'clock.

The next place that I was to journey was to the bus stop again I had got on the bus

which was heading for the town, on the journey I had met another girl her name was Alex she was becoming a friend closer than any of my spiritual lovers, brothers, and sisters. she was skinny I did not have an issue with that. I looked out of the window. What did I notice about the outside it had become of less green there was sometimes a lot of green but it looked out of place it seemed to me that the whole planet was made of concrete pathways and dead trees and now I did not hear anybody say or mention their names? It was concrete. I was not trying change the planet, I looked again and again and again and it was true Alex was true all I could see was concrete the roads and houses.

I kind of lost my temper a bit and spoke out loud this caused a fight. with myself and Alex a verbal disagreement. Then my bus slowly entered the country side the passengers were getting more and more restless the smaller children on the bus started to bicker and crying came afterwards. The noise was unbearable but I had to laugh it off. It was not surprising that a fight broke out between two of the teenagers as it happens I was there to settle them down, it's always me I said to myself. I grabbed the first teenager who was really kicking off and told him to shut his mouth and sit down he did it straight away the other boy continued and was literally in tears. Then for no reason a girl in the back ground broke down and started crying too, nobody went to comfort her. It came to the point when just about everyone on the bus had tears in their eyes or was fully crying. I guess the experience was too much for her. When I looked around and down I found that myself on a bed with her. I was sitting on my bed legs stretched and crossed over. She was sitting the same legs crossed over and looked in deep meditation. I do not know if she was in deep meditation with style I did not ask her or try to wake her. I know now that I was not the only human who could know everything about everything and through my experiences. I was not going to share my experiences I was not going to doctors and I kept a clear view of what I was experiencing I was not about to give up. I sat down on my mat I closed my eyes I found out that the girl was extremely close to me it was the select the elite that I was coming to the conclusion that I must find a way of telling my soul the truth. That that I was dying that there was a conspiracy to murder me out of the circle which I had created. The cat, the present dent, my other self, they were all suspects in my mind oh yes and my flat mates, I could quite easily be on my own but I wanted to be with my friends. A reunion was what I had in mind a meeting of old friends and pals that I met on my journey that I had met through meditation through my mind. Many people say that the mind is a beautiful and great minds think alike. I was sure as hell not going to die and I made it clear to those who were following me.

I knew something was going on but I just chose to ignore it. But my wife who was a gambler and was bent and was trying to murder me. We fell out over gambling debt she sold my car to pay for it without my permission. She tried to approach me on several occasions she would do things like slipping a tea bags into my dinner that she cooked hoping that I would swallow it and choke to my death, but I knew there was a tea bag in it but I said nothing as it was petty I was not going to make a big fuss over it she only used to have dreams of murdering me. I could hear her in her sleep talking about it. I opened my eyes I could feel a presents I did not want to say a thing but it was a friend of a friend's dad. I tried to stop him but he was too powerful I was now using the words of wisdom and then a long prey. But he still persisted on entering my mind. He had my soul I had no choice but to talk to him. He was persistent in sucking the soul out of my mind. I tried to ween him off me but it was too late he was in my head.

Going back to my first premonitions of myself in the smokers hut I had to ask myself what was I doing there. The day had been long I had obverse everything that happened on that day, in that dream or meditation, meaning the vision of the vision of what you begin to visualize once you have found your destination or place of rest. In meditation the word merit was just made up so that it was easier for its players to remember. The names of places your soul went to visit, Then the little girl in the corner of my room said something to me it was so soft I could just about hear her. I asked her if she could repeat it again but she said it was too hard. She looked frighten by my approach. So I asked her if she was in danger she said no, I am not infecting that's when she said that it was pure sunlight she was after that's when her tone changed I knew it from somewhere It was my mother. So I asked the girl if she knew who she was there was silent for a minute or too. And then we both said together son she went on, so there I was a 38 yr. old man with a teenage mum how did that work out. I began to talk to her it was so real the more I spoke the more she laughed out loud and louder it lasted almost 5 minutes and it seemed like hours. Then time ran out and I had to return myself to myself.

All my friends had gone home I had travelled to three or four destinations in and through my meditations. I had only just met my mentor who was a teenage girl who happened to be my mother in her next life. So I had to ask myself where was my father. I had asked that question before, she walked around the room for a while then went to the window she was persistent in trying to change the subject her words were stuttered she became quite upset, I did not blame her. She them caught her breath after wiping the tears off her face. She tried to explain that my father could not be found and he was not from this planet and for a very long time she did not speak with him. I found the conversation up setting and I did not understand it until she said he would join us soon but she never said that if he did not finish his mission he would miss the opportunity. She said he would join us in the next haven and not in this one. Right from the beginning I knew that what I was doing I was controlling myself through different parts of the spiritual journey which would be the beginning of my next life I was not going to die this was merely the start of a new life I wanted to come back as me well what I mean is I would be me but I would have a new body I don't think I would come back as a new born but I always believed I would come back as a teenager tiresome, bad timing but witty. When I realized I had found a new body I am slightly going out of my depths here but I will continue I wanted to destroy it I could see what I was doing to myself was bad but I knew it felt good. I just said to myself.

had to have one more try I was stupid I knew that I was dead now God had explained everything he said that I was so good that he had to keep on redirecting me and this was my fifty forth resurrection I had or was finished working in haven it was only that I would have approach the main man himself and ask him if I could be resurrected as my actual self and try to make all the decisions myself. That I would put all the wrongs I did right and perfect my life so that one day I would live in haven again. It's all complicated I do not expect you to understand it. So back to the journey of being me. I could feel my body, it was toned to perfection I could feel my stomach it was muscular and my legs were well built too. The only problem I had was the first problem of the rest of my life again it was perfect I was being contacted and I knew straight away it was God he had decided to talk with me. He said he was leaving that he had had enough of the human race but we were not to be blamed for things like wars and global warming because it was all him he was behind it. I asked him by bowing my head while kneeling and saying nothing where to His reply at first was that he gave me an overwhelming stare his eyes that got bigger, I'm moving to the artic he said the polar bear needs me. Is there anything else I said what do you what me to do I said it was sad I could feel the tears build up in my eyes I did not want to think about it infect I just manage to get a hold of myself. For a long time, all I could think about was happy thoughts but something had come over me. While I was going through this slight transformation I looked up in front of me still bowed down to the Gods the big eyes which he had and as he raised up his arms in greatness he had on a big apparel, white and he appeared to be holding a wooden staff he was doing something to my soul. He gave an almighty tap of his staff onto the floor and my soul was raised up. And was filled with pure light with an another tap of his staff he filled me with all the knowledge of kingdoms of heaven and the earth. God had to change his clothes. I suggested a shirt and jeans he took off his white appeal and changed behind his throne he was talking to me as he changed. He had finished and said if I would not mind if he wore a sweat shirt rather than a shirt as was a little bit childish. I smiled and said that's fine. He bowed down and sucked his face in. I Really wanted to go with him. But my job now was to rule over the heavens. God past his staff to me and put a baseball

cap on his head. Then he disappeared I did not see him go and I had to double check. In my new body I had only sat down for a second a few minutes just to give myself a taster. I could have glided away I wanted to move fast I had a lot to offer and I had a lot of ideas. I was me knew body and I could feel my mind It was full again. I sat down in the position head up legs crossed. I found myself moving through my mind extremely fast it less than a spilt second and I also found that I could find anything whether it was an object or a human being. I had not been experimenting with my new mind for too long before I found her it was a little girl something had
 happened it was her mum she could not find her I said to the girl I would find her for her and I did she said thank you and clasped my hand.

All my friends had gone and I was the only one left I had travelled to three or four destinations in and through my meditations. I had only just met the girl was the reincarnation of my mother who incidentally was still alive. So I had to ask myself where was my father and what about if I was the only child I did not recall having brothers or sisters. Thinking about this made me feel upset. And after a while I had begun to cry I wiped the tears from my eyes with a hanky. The night was young and the could were apart in the sky the sun was slowly setting and it looked beautiful on the sunset. I had not been here on the planet for long I did not understand it until I heard a whisper in my left ear you have not finished your mission so you cannot join us at this particular moment then the voice said you can join us in the next haven or on earth the priests said. Right from the start I knew that I was controlling myself through the havens and stars hoping to find the ultimate journey, the buzz, the rush of the best spiritual journey which would be the beginning, the next life. I had not died I had merely continued my life elsewhere. In my new body, I had only sat down for a minute just to give myself a taster I could have glided myself straight in to heaven it's self but I did not want to rush things, I had other ideas.

The first person who I wanted to meet was the girl who was my mother. I was very eager to meet her so I sat down and crossed my legs. In me knew body as I did was filled with pure light and only to my surprise I found out that it was not my mum but it was her house which I was giving high praises too. In my mind or in that house something had happened. The little girl had gone also I could not find her. So I waited and I waited but nothing. I remember the things that she had told me, I was upset that I had only met with her once. I was on a journey I knew inside that I was beginning to find my actual self; I think that's what you would call it. If you were going to experience anything that I had experienced in the last four years or so that it reminds me to tell you of these assurances, it did not happen overnight. I was getting closer to my destination as the time slowly past that when I got a message the same voice in the same ear like a soft breeze tickling my sides. I was going to meet my father and as a teenager I was surprised that I could not speak with them both together. It all came down to this conclusion I had to figure out this predicament I had met my mother on a plain when she was a little girl and I met my grown up father in an another life as a teenager, but I had no mum as a teenager and why could not find my father on this plane. I did not want to bother myself with the thought. It was clearly a sore point.

After we had played together we sat down both in my vision I politely asked him for a drink then I realized that it he was a she the only reason that I thought this was because she was a man was both woman and men wear the same white apparel. So I sat down on their plane, they had made sure that I was made welcome they showed me in gifts they had some and now had some. I wondered around for a while I felt quite lost. I had not traveled this far out of my mind before and I think I lost my way abet. I did not want to tell anybody about but with the amount of meditation that I had done I should have been able to find

 my way back. I found it a little bit embarrassing. That's when I had a vision so powerful that if I had spoken about it would have upset the heavens. The vision was of a past life it was my actual actual life somebody had attempted to murder me it was only a small vision but its power was fourth score. That was the thought. I have never forgotten the feeling of being hurt and feeling hurt in just one moment in all my life. And I was sickened by this. And from that day I asked the lord to stay by my side. I was getting tired then out of the corner of my eye I saw a lonely figure it was coauthoring around it was in hell. I came across as friendly but I had to many problems the girl who has no name looks at things in an over serious way. She says that she is a friend through all the meditations that I have done I could sincerely say that she has a problem excepting herself and the truth. What was the TRUTH. I know after experiencing this the truth had died. Saying the word truth was reminding of the little girl I met and it was filling her without light. I could see her standing there.

I did not want to disturb her so I got down on one knee and said a prayer wishing her the best of luck. That's when I realised that I had to get knack to normal life. It had been four years since I had left my consciousness we had travelled through the eye to many places.

The scariest Australia, the most loved in England, The most fear some of the plans of Africa on to the continent of America. That was where my family was all the knowledge sucked into me. The father I travelled the more gained knowledge I have travelled across the earth and universe with the four highest heavenly beings which God has sent me. Saints, angels, brothers and princes they have all been my guides and my friends. When I awoke I found myself in my bed there were some people standing by the bed they were all nattering. I looked around the room I could clearly see that I was being spoken to by some very important people I could see two men they were tall and they lent over me they introduced themselves as the two kings there was a little boy he announced himself as the prince. There was a short silence then the boy prince spoke "we have become great friends they commanded",

My opinion always varied but to them was valued. They explained that they had been there all of the time. And that they had been travelling with me from the start of my meditations. They said that they had been watching over me. That was the end of the adventure and a new adventure was about to arise. This

Chapter 14 The lost

time it began with my pen, I picked it up and started writing I was writing about everything which I had experienced
the words were just flowing out of me it was like a water fall of words which echoed around me I was excited. First of all, I thought my writing was rubbish for some time but it all made sense in the first place. I had to write about healing and mediation. It was not impossible to turn off the mind, I've seen it done. It takes a tablet or two but it works.
At last I was being to see it was the fifth year all was well there was one place which I wanted to see desperately and that was the underneath of the ocean. What was down there I asked myself. I took the matter up with the princess her answer to that was well we do own the oceans as well. I aged but I knew that GOD would take the Oceans back.

The princess asked me if I was ready I replied yes she took my hand and in a split second we were there in under the sea. I can explain the feeling that I was experiencing the water was warm the water ran fast it rushed past me as I was hit by some
turbulence. For a moment I had lost her visually as I was being swept away the water began to drag us apart, For the next couple of minutes I stayed in deep meditation it seemed like hours.

When I had finished I asked the princess if she had experienced the same. On the contrary I saw everything that you experienced and you were by my side. She replied. And the brothers about us agreed also, I still could not believe it was like everything was falling back into place. I watched out for accessibly I already knew that she was my wife and I was married to her. Because I have the qualities I was quite forgiving and I had good qualifications. I suppose you could say that about anybody but these were not ordinary people. As time the people only chose to meet on planes. As we grew apart our love for each other grew stronger and stronger until it had bonded and tied itself back together.
 For the power and love our lord God had given you and me was no mistake. It was so powerful that God himself had to bless it and enter the spirit, he was blessing the planet and the solar system. They needed a new name for planet earth. The earth was growing and its name was undecided. Everything was well I stood up I ached all over my body I had lost a considerable amount of weight. I hobbled off to kitchen. The pain grew quickly. It had started in my legs and ran up through me to my body then I reached my face finally. I began to cry my tears were not like normal tears I had big tears. I was sad, we all were. I could still see a few things. The expression on my face as I was told was sort of happy and then sad and looked as if I was going to laugh. The pain eventually subsided and the feelings in my body went back too normal. I was seeing things made of pure light, and blue. What I was going to experience next was the knight hood I was given three gifts the first was my mediation and imagination. But Before I was given the knight hood I had to pick a quarrel with the king and queen to see if I was holy enough I lost I was beaten by my wife and the king and queen but my wife stood by me. We had shared quite a lot since we had met we had even cried together once or twice she never lost her temper as I showed her my emotions as she showed me hers, I got down on my knees

and said a prey. I filled my eyes with light and my soul came back to me it was something that I worried about the most, my meditation even though now I was getting good at it I still made mistakes it was like a job interview you do not open your mouth until you are asked the questions in my case I was a bit hasty and wanted to know everything in such a short period of time it's like your dinner you eat it very slowly even if you have not got a lot. To me it was like time travel I could be near or far away and think nothing of it although I tended to stick to the same places going back and forth depending on how far I had walked on that day. Meditation became my life even more so I had prey. I would just sit there and prey all day long forgetting now actually how dangerous it could be but I kept a limit on things, or I would simply meditate. Prey brought me excitement and took me to places I did not know a lot about prey but it kept my soul contempt with everything. The hardest thing possible about all of this was how I was going to keep the peace it was an ongoing trust a pact between myself and God and I choose to keep it with him. I had been summoned to the throne I knew that the king wanted to test me I walked in I felt a cold breeze the hair stood up on my neck with excitement.

bow your head I was given a nudge and prompted so I did so. I said it although I was not asked a question I was about to say to the question but the true answer was yes I wanted the crown I could not help myself after a long period of thought I was beginning to think about writing some of my experiences down so I did it I wrote the book. The book sold about half a million copies on the first day I was rich it explained everything that I experienced in this book. At the end of my journeys I met with my brother we sat and discussed just about everything that there was to discuss the evening ended with a cup of tea.

I had not seen her for about three months. In the morning it was a usual routine for me down to the bus stop, I grabbed what I could hoping that I would miss my house mates and my brother s early morning banter about me being lazy. I began to think about how all this meditation started.

If I was not so popular my best friends would have not tried to remove me but they tried and they tried real hard living without my spirit was quite hard some people say the spirit is murderous other say you need to feel the spirit it exists around you and in you.

My wife knew me well by now and she invited me outside to watch the sunset. It was extremely tranquil blue. In the olden days the sun would have been a bright yellow color and the set a crimson red. Talking about the sun made me think of the

ink of the last part of the story. Everybody was in place we were all sitting in the dining area there was a large white table with large clear glasses it was quite a shock when I found out what they were serving. There were three plates in front of me. On the plate was a meal, it was in two special tablets and there was a knife and a fork I sat at one end of the table with my wife the princess at the other I leant over the speaker to so I could press the button to speak to her

"is this it."

she replied "just eat it please."

I said nothing the tablets were quite hard and large it was green and white. It was a capsule. I dabbled with it on my plate with my knife and fork. I could not cut the food in half, so I swallowed it whole. There was nothing for a minute or two then the strangest tastes came to my mouth it was stupendously delicious in fact it was fantastic, fabulous and delightful.

"it's great I said.

That was the last time I saw the princess. I had finally awoken Dave was standing over me "yes he is back   you've been out for a quite a while I vet got all of your messages your agents been worried sick you have got a tone of mail oh yes you got the lead part in the film you were talking about".

I answered him quaintly "well I am the best go on clap and applauded".

"you don't look too happy".

"No I mean yes I'm over the moon".

"you start tomorrow evening".

The next day came around quickly I had no time to prepare myself for the

part, which in my case was frustrating I explained the problem to Dave as I went through the script. I managed to pick up the first four parts. I spoke to my agent we agreed that I should just make the rest up and hoped that the director would except whatever came out of my mouth. I was pretty good at my job I could hit a scene with one to three lines in a second so making the rest of the script up would not be a problem. Well it was time to go to the set. Dave was driving me there we got into the car he asked me if I had everything. Pops I have forgotten the script. We went back inside I had left it on the kitchen side I pick it up it was as heavy as the bible and as thick as the works of Shakespeare. We go back into the car, he asked me what time we had to be there I think my agent said ten a clock what's the time he did not answer me straight away. We won't be late I know a short cut to the studio we will miss the morning traffic. I did not reply. There was a short silence I asked Dave if he would put the car radio on he said yes on with the music, so we started the journey I felt kind of dreamy everything I looked at seem not real the scenery looked false like it was fake and I felt a weird feeling a good weird feeling there was a tingling in my feet and

chapter17 missing you

then it went straight up to my arm. Break a leg that's the spirit that's what I thought it was good luck to say that. I looked out of the window it was I would say different I was watching the people walk by some of them looked pour others looked rich I was pretty rich and I was thankful. It just made you think about the divide in society I was so glade I was not pour. I did not want to close my eyes I did not want to miss a thing I was taking everything in. people, cars, old biddy's, women everything that I saw I was thankful for. Dave was not speaking which was not unusual, he was concentrating on the journey, he was a good driver and fast to. He loved his car in fact as I thought of this he just put the foot down I opened   the window and stuck out my head just to humor Dave. He drove one handed at about ninety miles' amour he lent his arm outside of the window like and LA gangster I think he did that because it was the cool way to drive. We pulled up to the traffic lights Dave slowly revved up the engine one minute and we were off again.
"Do you know where you are going".
"yeah I think so take a left at the bride groom shop I mean the wedding shop".
"Are yeah I've got you". He replied.
We were there Dave pulled up into the car park there was at least a hundred cars parked here there was no spaces I told Dave after looking for a space to just pull up right outside the main entrance, he did so.
We walked inside, it was like a cheap frill nobody recognized me. I understood this was not going to be a low budget film. After about twenty-minute s of greeting people. And meeting people. I met my agent and I was taken for the press review. This was brill we sat there at a table the cameras

streaming all over the place I walked in and sat down. There was a glass of water waiting for me I sat down and met the rest of the cast. The camera's started it was amazing I did not have to say a word. Clicking and the flashing of the camera lights was all I could see. That lasted for about ten minutes then there was silence that's when the press asked the first question. It was not for me the question but I answered it anyway the guy next to me gave me a nudge I then realized what I had done and apologized the camera kept on clicking away. I was given a chance to speak eventually

my voice was a little squeaky so I adjusted my throat and answered the question I could not believe it. I wiped the sweat from my brow it had run into my eyes so I had begun to squint I went for a glass of water but due to not being able to see because of the sweat in my eyes I spilt it all over the actor next to me he grunted and shouted what the hell do you think I was doing. I went to stand up as I did I caught the table cloth and pulled half of and what was on the table in front of me on to my lap and the floor. The camera clicked even more, I was busy apologizing the other actors and started laughing. It was quite funny I guess I then on purposely fell on the floor and quickly got up there was a cheer I took a bow and then poured myself another drink of water. Well that was the end of that the camera men slowly left I and was left alone the filming was going to start in a day or two I had accommodation at the studio. Me and Dave wanted to find the set, the studios were massive they had everything it was not as big as universal or warner brothers I would say it around or a bit bigger than pinewood studios. It did not take us long to find it was large. The set was massive everything was enlarged to fit the camera' s. I was looking for a chair with my name on it. When I found it I smiled it was a large director's chair it had my name on the back I jumped into it. Dave was busy taking photographs of set. I closed my eye s it felt high up and it held my weight I was only around thirteen stone I was wondering when the rest of the crew would turn up it was going to be a couple of hard nights and busy mornings. Dave had taken his last picture which was of me in the chair. Then he left I was on my own it was peaceful. I could smell the air it was sweet and somebody had left a bouquet of flower s and a bottle of beer for me. In the bouquet was a greeting card there was a message it read all the best break a leg and there was some lavender. Underneath the flowers was a box of chocolates. I did not open them or the bottle of beer although as I felt fine it gave me something to focus on the next morning, I awoke to the sound of a truck and the director's car had also pulled up the other members of the cast had just awoken it was funny but everybody turned up at the same time. I did not see the win bagel last night but there was three of them one of them was mine. The director was an odd looking fellow he was wearing a big jacket with shorts and sandals. I introduced myself his reply to my introduction was yes I know who you are this guy would set me on fire it was not going to be easy working for him I had now taken this into account. It was a dog eat dog world and he was the Rottweiler and I was the chewawa. I picked up the bottle beer opened it and took a sip a big sip. The director was getting his stuff together. He called out I want everybody on the set in fifteen. He ment fifteen minutes I closed my eye' s once more too ready myself. I put the bottle down on the table the other actors turned up and got into their seats two minutes later the whole crew had turned out. The crew was massive there was people everywhere. The adrenaline pumped through my body. I was all sweaty I wiped my brow I was pretty fit the sun was just coming out and the dew on the ground was rising into air making a soft fog. I came over light headed that was the beer I was a light weight.

The filming had begun there was silent not a sound was to be made it was so quiet I could hear my self breathe I had the main role but I was not introduced into the film until the third scene. The filming went on it was almost tiring just watching it the cast that I was working with were right armatures the first guy who's name I can't recall had a stutter it was half a day gone before

he had captured his style and it took eighteen takes I could see the rest of the cast doing the same. I was not board but I could not bear to watch this pour guy any more I went off the set to find my win bagel.

It took me five minutes to find it and about half an hour to figure out where the keys were to get in. They were underneath the box of chocolates which were left for me with another note it read have a smashing day and best of luck and break a leg. It was not signed. I let myself in, it was quite spacious it had everything laptop, TV, Games console, and the kitchen was stacked with beer, wine and food in the fridge was milk and cheese. Great I thought. I wanted to meditate but I decided not to matter of principal never mix work with pleasure. I turned on the game's console this was unreal the computer game was the film that I was staring in I had to ask myself the question when was the script written because it was a computer game as well. I was never any good at games so I just grabbed myself a beer and sat down on the sofa and put my feet up on the table casually. I did not feel tired but I just felt that I should go to sleep the armature actors were going to take all day I could tell. It was hot for one and two I wanted another beer and I wanted to crash out. I was on the bed for about five say ten minutes tossing and turning I could not sleep it was too hot for one and two I was too excited I got up and went for a walk. I got up and walked out of the win bagel I left the door open. The film studio was huge I did not know where to start not the pub and there was one I could have gone to the theme park it seemed fun enough but I did not fancy it. I breathed the fresh air into my mouth and exhaled the freshness of the air cleansed my soul. The fog had disappeared and it looked like it was going to be a nice day but just as I said this to my self the sun went in and it came over cloudy this always happens to me. I took my mobile phone out of my jacket pocket and checked the weather report that was funny according to the weather report on my phone it's going to be sunny all day.

You can never believe the weather report I guess. I made it back to the main set, the director had just finished giving the actor his directions his loud voice had an echo to it he demanded that there was quiet on the set just like all directors do. I made it to my chair I picked up the bottle of beer which was open and sipped from. And watched. It was going to be a long day I could tell. Then out of the blue I got a text it was Eugene the text which is a message electronically sent through to you via your phone it said best of luck and break a leg kiss, kiss, kiss that made my day I texted her back straight away. I wrote, Hello babe having a great time but these actors are armature. She texted me back almost straight away.

I have got his car, house, oil, everything, the guy that I was playing, he was some flash dummy from America.

He had a pair of eights, I had nothing I was bluffing, he thought for a while I thought he had something and he folded.,"

"Well you All the promotions around twenty million

CHAPTER 18 The big film

"that's a hell of a lot of loot, I'm your best friend."

"I know".

"Know I mean it".

"Eugene made five hundred thousand on the cat walk Yesterday she got a check and on top of that she got another three hundred thousand for the movie".

"I on the other hand made seven and a half million on a game of blackjack I bluffed my way right from the start

you look good".

"Okay that's enough about money".

"Well that's all good news what's on the TV". In the evening, we laughed, cried and eventually went to bed.

The next morning, I walked into the living room

"what's going on here."

   "hay "

   "hi".

I jumped into the arm chair it was my chair. It was my chair and nobody sat in my chair it was house rules.

And the second was that nobody disturbs me while the footballs on.

"well" I said, there was a pause "how is everybody".

"so Dave how did it really go".

"It went really well how much did you really make?".

"After tax and agent's fees".

"obviously"

"Sorry I cannot tell you it is not that I do not want to tell you it is too hard to account after all the promotions and TV. The film its self-will properly makes a hundred million in the next year".

I was the lead a method actor.

It would have been really good if Eugene could have known my child, Anyway I Had to get home there was something that I had to do I had to spend more time with Dave and Eugene or they would suspect something. So we spent a few more days loving the house which I was trying to sell. My mum came over to she was a funny old lady. I kept on playing the same old joke but she never caught.   It was how does she like her tea in the morning. She never caught on. It was Wednesday I told the others that I had enough over a game of twister you know that old on the floor board game. I walked trying to look necked as If I was about to pass out and went to my bedroom. I thought that they had sassed me out when I was called back but I politely declined. If they found out that all I did was sleep all day I mean how much sleep and rest does the actor need.

I transcended back into the journey it was colorful there was a huge forest that kept on coming into my mind me and the princess had spoken about it. I wanted to be with her all the time I was in love with her, just her appearance, and she was always polite to her people she was a giver of life like a water fall forever flowing with knowledge she was forgiving we had often spoke about bathing there, there was a river close by.

I had just awoken I was woken by the TV it took me a few second s to gather my soul and mind I got up and got dressed I put on a shirt which I left untucked, a jumper, brief, socks and jeans in that order, I stood by my bedroom window for a minute.

Everybody was in the great hall in the palace that's all I could see it was like being famous twice over once on the earth and the second on the plane. The Cat had the camera and it was taking pitchers of all the people who were dancing, cheering and clapping. You name it, it was a great celebration. There were all kinds of kind people here in the palace. I was about to take my eye off the Cat when I looked up. Then all I could see was the president and 23 stuffing their faces. The food was of the highest quality although it was very small in stature as you already know. There were children running everywhere in the hall ways and jesters juggling and people having a good time.

On the next day I awoke in her arms half a sleep on the dining table I was still in the palace. Eugene, I had thought of her for the first time I had crated this all of this by chance it was the first time that I thought of inviting my friends into my world, there was no way I was going to give them up.

The presedent was there he said to me look at this letter again please, the message had changed he asked if it was my doing. 23 returned my job to me. It was like I had become extremely powerful and it was said that I was a teacher and should be watched day and night.

In the next days the Cat had tried to befriend me again for the second time he claimed was just being a Cat and he said that he desperate to get his body back. He was searching for a body like mine. He laughed a lot while we spoke about this it was proberly true but I have my doubts.

Although I thought that everything was going good all the time my luck was about to change it started first thing in the next morning I had a letter. The postman came up to the door he knocked loudly and waited. I was a bit slow to answer the door I had a letter it was marked special delivery. I just caught him as he was just turning away.
"Hi there how are you doing "I put my American accent just to impress him.
"your mail". he said.
"Cheers have a nice day". I replied I was in a rush to open it the envelope I mean in it was the letter. Ripping it open I found a letter it was a messy opening for my standards the paper was torn completely the president. IT was said that the president was going to visit me tonight. I know that the president and the 23 were extremely powerful he was more than my job was worth in fact the letter it explained that there had been a new arrival and my job had been done the only thoughts were of my son would I ever see them again.

Eleven thirty I sipped coffee from a mug in the kitchen I was on my own which was not unusual. The next thing which was about to change was the meditation I had lost the power to meditate I had been cut off. I sat down I had not realized at first I crossed over my legs I was already stripped down and I had closed my eyes there was nothing I tried again. And nothing,
"weird" I said.
I tried it on standing up so I did and nothing again. I had one more chance I played down on the floor keeping my cool I closed my eyes it was bang on twelve o'clock the clock in the hall way clock chimed. Again my mind did not move I walked to my bedroom opened the door since I had been meditating I had a voice activated door lock on my bedroom door so nobody would disturb me. I sat on my bed and waited. I was just about to close my eyes when my mind came active again full on. It was cool It was different I could feel total peace and my mind was open. I could visualize everything I could see the princess sitting on her throne she spoke out. The term she used was that she was with me, then one of the seven I was told was approaching me I hovered up off the floor the power he welded was incredible he said his words to me where I am your son he put one hand on my shoulder then walk

away to join his mother at her side.

Then the Cat turned up.
"Still looking for a body cat"
I called out again.
I have not forgotten what you did Cat.
The cat swiveled and turned around and went and stood beside my son.

I did not smoke often but really fancied a ciggy I put my hands deep into the pocket of my jacket I could feel everything lose change, at the first touch I could feel some money then my second feeling was my lighter, then nothing. I began to pat myself down searching desperately for my cigarettes. Then I remembered that they were down stairs on the bottom of the stair case inside the pocket of my other jacket. So down stairs I went skipping down the stairs I had found what I was looking for. I had to smile. While I was smoking this fine cigarette. I decided to think about God. It was God that gave me the gift of meditation, then something strange happened I went to put the cigarette out still thinking about God I went back upstairs in to one of my bedrooms and stood looking at my mirror I

Chapter19 B

was posing when I burnt myself with my cigarette it was not so painful at first but then I notice that the flesh under health my skin was white this gave me the conclusion that the whole world was white and color was just another test, this gave me an idea I
had to meditate again I had to find the president and 23

Somehow all this meditation slowly beginning to add up and going back to the very start of my story everything that I learnt. The meeting
of the Cat I hate to mention its name, the president and 23, the tramp, the corpse who is my dead father myself, the princess, Dave, Eugene were all inter linked. I was coming to the conclusion that it was for the fight for world spiritual peace. In all of this the only person who I had not seen was the devil and I was not too keen on meeting him and we all know he is about. Maybe he did not have time for me. There were many stories of me members who had lost their minds while traveling around their own body's and their souls

were taken and destroyed the princess spoke of this. So it was import ant that I send out the right message after that conversation with my consciousness throwing the devil out had left me quite harmonious and peaceful, I had not said a prey for a while as I was caught in two worlds. Through meditation was a kind of prey. I had not been down on my knees to thank God I was about to do so. My son was growing up fast he was growing up and I was growing younger. This pleased the princess and myself to watch him grow it was

a little miracle he was a miracle it the greatest miracle it was a real gift and should be nurtured and loved to the highest level every single ounce of it should be loved. Children can be funny. A friend of mine once said a child could be more intelligent than its bearers so watch out. But a child will follow to learn, they can be greedy and tormented

 hateful they are pretty good lyres too. But they can be extremely honest and they will always need love I guess everybody does in the end. They can be powerful to that's why we use them on this planet in our world children are sacred. Any way that's enough about that I thought.

My next actions were to get drunk I had not be drunk for quite a while tell a small lie I had a drink last winter when I was on the film set. I walked down stairs to my study I expected to meet Eugene on the way. I stubble as I entered the room I was not drunk yet. I was looking for a bottle of champagne but it was not there right I said to myself I'll have to go down to the wine cellar so I did. There was always a bottle down there, the stairs were steep and the walls were cold to touch. I ran my hand down the wall to the bottom of the banister. I looked around I had a large collection as you already know it did not take me long to find another bottle of bubbly that's when I hesitated I was not sure whether I should take the bottle or not I looked up at the celling and pushed my hand down on the stairs as I climbed to the top. I put the bottle down on my drawing table. I sat down on my chair taking everything into my mind it felt weird just sitting there I had not done this for a while It felt quite good to this time I did not close my eyes.

He had made enough money from one card game to go back to work would you believe it card playing. we spoke he said he had won in the regions of five hundred thousand just in card games and he had a small fortune in a stash you know in case of emergencies of around four million. And how did I know about this well he left his phone on my table. It was one of those cheesy flip top one's kind of funny considering the circumstances. The tight get that explains why he chooses to keep his mouth shut.

I was feeling a light chill I wanted to get a fire started but it was getting a little late I stayed in the chair until the early hours of the morning. Passing in and out of consciousness   I did not get really get any sleep. Well as for a glass of champagne there was only so much in the end it was not worth it and I could not be bothered to go all the way down stairs I put the empty bottle down on the table and sat back in the arm chair it was so comfortable and I just sat there taking everything into my mind. It felt quite good just sitting there I had not done this for a while as I was always on the floor or standing up meditation or sitting down.

By the time I had woken up it was twelve o'clock, there was no point in getting up so I waited until about six pm. That's when I got off the sofa. I was feeling a little rough, I clambered into the shower. The water was hot it was soothing to and it felt good to feel the water touch my body. After seven minutes under the shower I grabbed the soap bar and started to wash seven minutes later I climbed out of the shower and began to dry myself on my towel. Now that I was dry I could wax my hair. I always waxed my hair once I was done I went and sat down in my director's chair. This was great there was nobody around I noticed a beer in front of me on a small table. There were some flowers on the table I could smell them. The set had changed too. That explained the the noise in the middle of the night. This time on the set there was a bed and this was the final scene. I was going to die while making love the scene goes me and this girl in the film have a fling the husband walks in and sees us together then he shoots her she's on top that's great. There was blood everywhere. Good tomato ketchup.

There were around 53 scenes in this production it was a short film with a big budget, why I was there. I was in the last eight scenes that means there was four scenes to go as I had just finished meditated. The film in its self was good it was getting more and more exciting as each scene passed.

It had been a good and hard year and a half. I had not meditated for a while now, but my other self-kept me in focus,

and told me what was going on with my son. The word was that he was growing up fast and he had already found a plane. I wondered about my other self he always said follow him but when I did he would shy away always trying to hide his face or hide behind objects like tables and chairs and more often the curtains and he was always doing things with his hands like jigsaws or knitting. The other day I saw him knitting a jumper it was for me. But then the thought captured my mind. Who was the real father of this child?

I looked down at cigar that I was smoking it was near its end a couple more puffs, the sensation of the smoke was too strong for me it was quite unbearable but I finished it off with ease. I threw the end of the cigar which was called the butt on to the floor and stamped on it hard into the ground. Then I picked it up off the floor and put it in my pocket.

Back at the mobile unit I had left my music on there was nothing left for me to do. I walked into my dressing room and I fell asleep rather quickly.

The next morning, I awoke early it was the 42dnd scene was at hand I knew it was the forty second scene because I had

Chapter20 Ghost walking

read the script fully. By now I had leant my lines it was going to be my turn again soon. I was a break dancer and people came from all over to watch I was good. The burn is what we called it, I was dressed in a red tracksuit and an old school pair of trainers. The first line was "my father never brought me anything and it was all my mother's money and that was not a lot".

The second line was that "my father was a tight get he keep every penny for himself the third line was "I have seen him in the next life. The part went on and on and as I did I got better and better. The lines flowed out of me putting me into a better mood the feeling was incredible. Then nothing, silence. and then an applauded.

With All the promotions there was around twenty million

"that's a hell of a lot of loot, I'm your best friend."

"I know".

"Know I mean it".

"Eugene made five hundred thousand on the cat walk Yesterday she got a check and on top of that she got another three hundred thousand for the movie".

"I on the other hand made seven and a half million on a game of blackjack I bluffed my way right from the start

I've got his car, house, oil, everything he was some flash dummy from

America.

He had a pair of eights I had nothing, he thought I had something and he folded.,"

"Well you look good".

"Okay that's enough about money".

"Well that's all good news what's on the TV in the morning, we laughed, cried and eventually went to bed.

The next morning, I walked into the living room

"what's going on here."

"hay "

"hi".

I jumped into the arm chair it was my chair. It was my chair and nobody sat in my chair it was house rules.

And the second was that nobody disturbs me while the footballs on.

"well" I said, there was a pause ". how is everybody".

"so Dave how did it really go".

"It went really well how much did you really make?".

"After tax and agent's fees".

"obviously"

"Sorry I cannot tell you it is not that I do not want to tell you it is too hard to account after all the promotions and TV and the film its self-will properly makes a hundred million in the next year".

I was the lead.

It would have been really good if Eugene could have known my child, any way I Had to get home there was something that I had to do I had to spend more time with Dave and Eugene or they would suspect something. So we spent a few more days loving the house which I was trying to sell. My mum came over to she was a funny old lady. All I kept on saying as a joke was how does she like her tea she never caught on. It was Wednesday I told the others that I had had enough over a game of twister you know that old on the floor board game I walked trying to look necked as If I was about to pass out to my bedroom. I thought that they had sassed me out when I was called back but I politely declined. If they found out that all I did was sleep all day I mean how much sleep does the actor need.

I transcended back into the journey it was colorful there was a huge forest that kept on coming into my mind me and the princess had spoken about it. I wanted to be with her all the time I was in love with her just her appearance and she was always polite to her people she was a giver of life like a water fall forever flowing with knowledge she was forgiving we had often spoke about bathing there, there was a river close by.

I had just awoken I was woken by the TV it took me a few seconds to gather my soul and mind I got up and got dressed put on a shirt which I left untucked, a jumper, brief, socks and jeans in that order, I stood by my bedroom window for a minute.

Everybody was in the great hall in the palace that's all I could see it was like being famous twice over once on the earth and the second on the plane. The Cat had the camera and it was taking pitchers of all the people who were dancing, cheering and clapping. You name it, it was a great celebration. There were all kinds of kind people here in the palace. I was about to take my eye off the Cat when I looked up all I could see was the president and 23 stuffing their faces I looked back down The food was of the highest quality although it was very small in stature as you already know. There were children running everywhere in the hall ways and jesters juggling and playing with the fire eaters.

On the next day I awoke in her arms half a sleep on the dining table I was still in the palace. I had forgot to meditate myself back as I was so drunk from the night before. I had thought of Eugene for the first time in ages I had crated this all of this by chance. It was the first time that I thought of inviting my friends into my world, I was not sure I knew that the princess knew what I was thinking although I wanted more time to think about this there was no way I was going to give them up just yet.

The president was there he said to me look at this letter again please, the message had changed he asked if it was my doing. 23 returned my job to me. It was like I had become extremely powerful and it was said that I was now a teacher and should over the day and night.

In the next days the Cat had tried to befriend me again for the second time he claimed was just being a Cat and he said that he desperate to get his body back. He was searching for a body like mine. He laughed a lot while we spoke about this it was properly true but I have my doubts that he will find one.

Although I thought that everything was going good all the time my luck was about to change. It started first thing in the next morning I had a letter. The postman came up to the door he knocked loudly and waited. I was a bit slow to answer the door I had a letter it was marked special delivery. I just caught him as he turned his back.
"Hi there how are you doing ". put my American accent just to impress him.
"your mail". he said.
"Cheers have a nice day". I replied I was in a rush to open it the envelope I mean in it was the letter. I ripped it open I found a letter it was a messy opening for my standards the paper was torn completely the president. It was said that the president was going to visit me tonight. I know that the president and the 23 were extremely powerful he was more than my job was worth in fact the letter it explained that there had been a new arrival and my job had been done the only thoughts were of my son would I ever see them again.

Eleven thirty I sipped coffee from a mug in the kitchen I was on my own which was not unusual. The next thing which was about to change was the meditation I had lost the power to meditate again I had been cut off. I sat down I had not realized at first I crossed over my legs I was already stripped down and I had closed my eyes there was nothing I tried again. And nothing, "weird" I said.
I tried it on standing up so I did and nothing again. I had one more chance I played down on the floor keeping my cool I closed my eyes it was bang on twelve o'clock the clock in the hall way chimed and again and again and again my mind did not move. I walked to my bedroom opened the doors since I had been meditating I had a voice activated door lock on my bedroom door so nobody could disturb me. I sat on my bed and waited. I was just about to close my eyes when my mind came active again full on. It was cool It was different I could feel total peace and my mind was open. I could visualize everything I could see the princess sitting on her throne she spoke out. The term she used was that she was with me, then one of the seven I was told was approaching me I hovered up off the floor the power he welded was incredible he said his words to me where I am your son he put one hand on

my shoulder then walk away to join his mother at her side.

Then the Cat turned up.
"Still looking for a body cat"
I called out again.
I have not forgotten what you did Cat.
The cat swiveled and turned around and went and stood beside my son.

I did not smoke often but really fancied a ciggy I put my hands deep into the pocket of my jacket I could feel everything lose change, at first touch I could feel some money then my second feel was my lighter, then nothing. I began to pat myself down searching searching desperately for my cigarettes Then I remembered that they were down stairs on the bottom of the stair case inside the pocket of my other jacket. So down stairs I went running down the stairs I had found what I was looking for. While I was smoking this fine cigarette. I decided to think about God. It was God that gave me the gift of meditation, then something strange happened I went to put the cigarette out still thinking about God I went back upstairs in to one of my bedrooms and stood looking at a wall mirror I was posing when I burnt myself with my cigarette it was not so painful at first but then I notice that the flesh under health my skin was white this gave me the conclusion that the whole world was white and color was just another test, this gave me an idea I
had to meditate again I had to find the president and 23 me ask them about what I had stubble upon and if they agreed.

Somehow all this meditation and going back to the very start of my story everything that I learnt. The meeting
of the Cat I hate to mention its name, the president and 23, the

Chapter21 I guess

tramp, the corpse who is my dead self, the princess, Dave, Eugene and myself were all inter linked. I was coming to the conclusion that it was for the fight for world spiritual peace. In all of this the only person who I had not seen was the devil and I was not too keen on meeting him and we all know he is about. Maybe he did not have time for. There were many stories of me members who had lost their minds while traveling around their own body's and their souls were taken and destroyed. So it was import ant that I send out the right message with after that conversation with my consciousness throwing the devil out had left me quite harmonious and peaceful, I had not said a prey for a while as I was caught in two worlds. Through meditation was a kind of prey. I had not been down on my knees to thank God I was about to do so. My son was growing up fast he was growing up and I was growing younger. This pleased the princess and myself to watch him grow it was

a little miracle he was a miracle it the greatest miracle it was a real gift and should be nurtured and loved to the highest level every single ounce of it should be loved. Children can be funny. A friend of mine once said a child could be more intelligent than its bearers so watch out. But a child will follow to learn, they can be greedy and tormented

hateful they are pretty good lyres too. But they can be extremely honest and they will always need love I guess everybody does in the end. They can be powerful to that's why we use them on this planet in our world children are sacred. Any way that's enough about that I thought.

My next actions were to get drunk I had not be drunk for quite a while tell a small lie had a drink last winter I was on the film set. I walked down stairs to my study I expected to meet Eugene on the way. I stubble as I entered the room was not yet drunk I was looking for a bottle of champagne but it was not there right I said to myself I'll have to go down to the wine cellar so I did. There was always a bottle down there, the stairs were steep and the walls were cold to touch. I ran my hand down the wall to the bottom of the banister. I looked around I had a large collection as you already know it did not take me long to find another bottle of bubbly that's when I hesitated I was not sure whether I should take the bottle or not I looked up at the celling and pushed my hand on the down onto the stairs. I put the bottle down on my drawing table in my study. I sat down on my chair taking everything into my mind it felt weird just sitting there I had not done this for a while It felt quite good this time I close my eyes.

He had made enough money from one card games to go back to work would you believe it card playing. We spoke he said he had won in the regions of five hundred thousand just in card games and he had a small fortune in a stash you know in case of emergencies of around four million. And how did I know about this well he left his phone on my table. It was one of those cheesy flip top one's kind of funny considering the circumstances. The tight get. I was feeling a light chill I wanted to get a fire started but it was getting a little late I stayed in the chair until the early hours of the morning. Passing in and out of consciousness I did not get really get any sleep. Well as for a glass of champagne there was only so in the end it was not worth it and I could not be bothered to go all the way down stairs I put the bottle down on the table and sat back in the arm chair it was so comfortable and I just sat there taking everything into my mind. It felt quite good just sitting there I had not done this for a while as I was always on the floor or standing up meditation or sitting down.

By the time I had woken up it was twelve o'clock, there was no point in getting up so I waited until about six pm. That's when I got off the sofa. I was feeling a little rough, I clambered into the shower. The water was hot it was soothing to and it felt good to feel the water touch my body. After seven minutes under the shower I grabbed the soap bar and started to wash seven minutes later I climbed out of the shower and began to dry myself on my towel. Now that I was dry I could wax my hair. I always waxed my hair once that was done I went and sat down in my director's chair. This was great there was nobody around I noticed a beer in front of me on a small table. There were some flowers on the table I could smell them. The set had changed too. That explained the noise in the middle of the night. This time on the set there was a bed and this was the final scene. I was going to die while making love the scene goes me and this girl in the film have a fling the husband walks in and sees us together then he shoots her she son top that's great. There was blood everywhere. tomato ketchup.

to it. There were around 53 scenes in this production it was a short film with a big budget, why I was there. I was in the last eight scenes that means there was four scenes to go as I had just fin meditated fished four. The film in its self was good it was getting more and more exciting as each scene passed.

It had been a good and hard year and a half. I had not meditated for a while now, but my other self-kept me in focus,

and told me what was going on with my son. The word was that he was growing up fast and he had already found a plane. I wondered about my other self he always said follow him but when I did he would shy away always trying to hide his face or hide behind objects like tables and chairs and more often the curtains and he was always doing things with his hands like jigsaws or knitting. The other day I saw him knitting a jumper it was for my child. But then the thought captured my mind. Who was the real father of this child?

I looked down at cigar that I was smoking it was near its end a couple more puffs, the sensation of the smoke was too strong for me it was quite unbearable but I finished it off with ease. I threw the end of the cigar which was called the butt on to the floor and stamped on it hard into the ground. Then I picked it up off the floor and put it in my pocket.

Back at the mobile unit I had left my music oh there was nothing left for me to do. I fell asleep rather quickly

The next morning, I awoke early it was the 42dnd scene was at hand I knew it was the forty second scene because I had

read the script fully. By now I had leant my lines it was going to be my turn again soon.

I was a break dancer and people came from all over to watch I was good. The burn is what we called it, I was dressed in a red tracksuit and an old school pair of trainers. The first line was "my father never brought me anything and it was all my mother's money and that was not a lot".

The second line was that "my father was a tight get he kept every penny for himself". The third line was "I have seen him in the next life and his poor, it did sadden me a lot.

I pulled the cigarette out of my shirt pocket and put one in my mouth. This is where I get frustrated I've lost my lighter again not to worry I do not get worried about things like that. I had a backup plan. I went into the studios kitchen, I thought it would be a good idea to light it off one of the cookers. It could work so I did two minutes later I found my lighter. Better luck next time I guess. I took a deep breath and a puff of the fag the taste was strong I mean really strong. I went back to my accommodation when I got into the van I was looking at a picture of my dad

"so dad ". I said to the picture "how poor are we".

There was now answer "oh the strong silence type".

I said it again holding the picture down only expecting that in some way some kind of immaculate conception would speak but nothing. That's when I realized that he was really gone. Somehow just touching the picture brought all the emotions back My eyes filled up with tears but I fought it and fought it well. I was not going to waste my tears on him. I turned the picture over then I hesitated and turned the picture back over then I told it that I had no time for tears and I was sorry. I turned the Music on lent back in my chair and took my mind off it.

I knew something was missing I loved listening to music I always thought that I would be a dancer of some sort but that's a whole different story.

It begins way in the eighties I had put the money ventures down and turned to hip hop.

I took my hand off and pushed the open the door just next door was a couple of drunk actors they were stubbing outside their van. I could not see who it was but it sounded like the other two lead actors who have main parts with me.

They were definitely having fun. All I could hear was laughter. I looked away in shame and shyness then went back inside I took my cap and jacket off and just looked at the table on the table was a pad some pens a candle stick holder some snacks and a drug prescription a bowl and to remote control. It was not

easy working on a film set this big you had to know where everything is although I was well catered for also on the table was a picture of my dad he was a royal engineer when he was alive he was a solider I did not really like him I suppose that amounts for something as he spent most of the time beating up my mother and spending most of his life in pub.

Well now I am all grown up and the silly money adventures have become serious make or break discussions
everything was going great anyway and I think on the money kind of things I am now even more comfortable it may seem. I got up and laid back father onto the sofa. I was tired and just wanted to go to sleep but I knew that something would disturb my cheeks, more visions and dream, the dreams I could not stand. I walked up to the door in the bedroom the air was hot and the beer that I had been drinking had become stale there was a sign on the door with my name on it. I tried to smudge it off with my fingers then my hand my name I thought on a pluck I thought that it was great but annoying

So I had just finished another film it went really well but there's more to come promotions and advertisements.

advertisements, sponsorship, I should make a clear two million then there's fees it's great. I have always liked money. Being Part of the film industry I don't often tell people about the shares I own as I also own the biggest TV company in the world and I also own a film studio amongst other things you are properly wondering how I made so much money. Well it started on guy's folk's night I had nothing to do so I made a guy it was made of old newspapers I played it down on the street between a pub and a corner shop. That was the start of my money making adventure. After this I became a carol singer as I recall it was Christmas I knocked on every house in the village that I was brought up in, it was on a council estate which me and my two brother were housed upon. I sang my nuts off for a whole week during the Christmas holidays and the reward for that was a large bag of money. After this it was down to the solders on the barracks where I lived I would wait until they passed me and then I would just stop to speak to them and during the conversation I would ask them for some money. I made enough money on that day to buy myself some sweets. This went on for about a year or so.
But my most favorite adventure was to selling holly. There was a holly tree in the park it took all evening cutting holly from its bush bagging it and selling it. That was good all of my little money making ideas and I have not been able to stop making money today. I do not spend out on everything sometimes I choose to go without things such as tooth paste, clothes, but in saying that the cars are in the garage but I have no silence.

It was night the sky was clear and the stars were out. I opened the front and back doors to let the light fresh air in. I looked around I was amazed just being here on the earth it was a real frill. I could not think of a better place to be, there was a bench in the garden so I walked over to it I sat down un did the buckles on my shoes and closed my eyes and praised the night I was there for a few hours I slowly fell asleep. When I awoke it was early morning there was due on the grass the sun was out I could clearly see it I was sweating I rubbed the sweat off my fore head and then wiped it off onto my knee. I then became extremely wide eyes and awake. I looked up to the clouds they were moving slowly and I watched the moon slowly recede back into space as the sun came out over powering the moon. The love that I could feel from the planet was incredible from the smallest thing to the largest plants they can love to it was like a dream. I came to the conclusion that I had everything the only thing left was for me to drive my car. I jumped up quickly and walked to my garage I already had the keys for my car on me.

As soon as I got back I took off my racing cap and threw it on the side as I walked into the house I had made quite a substantial amount of money I was thinking about selling the mansion for even more money. After everything that I gone through while being here I wondered if it would be worth it. I was still in love with the place. Although My place was good but old and dingy I was looking for something a little bit more modern.

I started to think about the idea of moving more and more. I had to tell the others to see what they would think and say of course I would take them with me. I always had a second opinion which I will be seeking in the near future. Even though it was early morning I decided to sleep through to The next day I woke up early in the morning it was hard trying to find enough sleep when you have so many demons. I slowly got up out of my bed and walked to my wardrobe I picked a shirt out and grabbed the first pair of jeans I could find. Socks, shoes, pants and vest

I went to the window while addressing that winter could be here soon I thought. I looked around the room I was looking for my sweets I had found them they had fallen behind the side cabinet. I had no idea how long they had been there but I needed to. I just wanted something to suck.

Eugene had awoken she explained to me that she had a really tough night she said in our conversation she said she had dreams of golden fields, I held here in my arms. While she tied back her blonde hair. She had a lot for a young person I was around ten years older than her. I stood her up on to her feet she was all floppy I looked at her face

face it she was like she was in a dream tears started pouring down her face they came down two by two both sides I said to her that I could not remember how many times that I had said this to her but you must know by now that we love you and I think that you are a little bit over worked. That's when the expression on her face changed I looked at her hard and gave her a kiss on her fore head. The crying did not stop there the more I tried to calm her the worst she got. I think she was in love.

Winter just around the corner I could feel the change in the air the wind had got colder and on some trees the leaves had fallen. Something was about change I did not know if it was me or the meditation. When I closed my eyes I could not see the planes that I would normally find I could not see the visions the light had become darkness. There was some new people who were entering my mind whatever it was not the rich presents anymore of a clean mind. My thoughts were racing instead of being calm these new people were dangerous. while I was getting a message from the others that were there. I meditated with the cat and the president. I was also being told to leave the plane to get outside to go anywhere but not into my own mind I was worried for my wife and son how would I see them. There were messages sent to me from a few people the cat and the president again but nothing from my son or my wife. I

Chapter23 Blind vision

began to realize that I had stubble upon pure evil it was not death or Satan it was nothing. I wanted to take my mind off things so I decided to do some reading I walked to my study. On the book self was books, comic books laden from top to bottom, such story's as back2back, the Hitman, Master criminal, many many other I had in the region of about two thousand. It took me around fifteen to twenty minutes to find a good comic. I found what I was looking for Spirits memory check, I dipped my hand into the shelf and pulled a couple of books. I jumped down off the ladder and into my chair and opened the first book and began to read it. The comic book script was put together quite well it read cross ways, it had bright colours and the charecters were red hot the story line too but that was normal. Boy meets girl, girl gets kidnapped, boy goes after girl and so on. It's the kind of thing I could read for hours I got so engrossed I forgot about the football this evening. The good thing about comic books is that they are never ending they can go on and on and on the way the characters change from time to time the story takes you on a terrible journey they are almost as good as a film script. I enjoy looking at the backs of the book there's always a picture of a super hero on them or the baddies as I call them. Every comic book I brought I actually read. As I recall this was the sixth time I had read this particular book and I still get excited.

What I also like about comic books is the little logo on the top left hand side, you always look at it for a minute before you open it. It is funny it was really quiet a good feeling, it was definitely a good wat to spend your time taking the hustle and the bustle of the world off your shoulders. In one story which was a tear jerker the main character dies. It kind of kills the rest of the story in the comic book.

I put the comic down that I was reading and picked up another. Now this looked good all the colors nice and bright but it was not unusual for comics to be brightly colored. I also like the characters in comic they sound all sound futuristic and not just this they have special super powers I would love to make a movie like this but I know and I see that it has already been done. I could imagine all my super heroes in a film it sounds good to me. Just think special effects, it would cost me a fortune and properly make me another one too.

Something extremely funny was about to happen as I lay there in my bed a robbery was at hand. That's right my beautiful home was about to be burgled. The whole place was belled up, but something went wrong with my alarm systems. There were rumors that there was a thief in the neighborhood it was all over TV and in the local papers. So I guess that why I keep on seeing police cars passing by my mansion, I shall continue it had just gone three o'clock in the morning, when I thought I heard somebody pass my bedroom door. This did not happen once but twice. I had to go and investigate it I picked up my tennis racket which was by the door gripping it tightly and opened the bedroom door gripping the bat even harder that's when I heard the footsteps, I knew it was an intruder because Eugene would have turned on the lights so would have Dave. That's when I heard the burglar's footsteps he was just going to leave. I ran down the corridor dropping the bat not realizing it's the adrenaline pumped through my body hands and arms in racing motion it was just as good as being in the movies. The adrenaline was pumping reaching out as I was spiriting around the corner into the main corridor and grabbing the thief who was now the victim. With both hands

As this happened Dave was just walking in too.

I've got him

what what s all the noise

don't move I said as I put the burglar in a head lock on the floor

    Dave turn on the lights I shouted

"what"
just do it let un mask this bandit
I could not believe it I pulled off the mask and to my surprise
"Darrell".
"who, who it's you".
"it is being it's you".
"I do not believe it."
"it's me ".
"it's you".
"I have not seen you for years are you still playing football".
" what the hell do you think you were doing".
"what me nothing".

"it does not look like nothing to me ".
Myself and Darrell had already been acquainted we played football together
for a couple of years at the local sports center way back in the day."
"I'll take those".
Dave grabbed the sack
"Dave hold on what's in the sack".
"My Rembrandt and oh my Mona".
"flip that's what it's called".
"and my Picasso".
"well what can I say I had fallen on hard times".
"I'd say Dave said joking".
"The kids had grown up the wife has left me I did not have much choice,
but you're doing alright though".
I interrupted him quickly.
"Would you like a beer".
"Go on then".
We walked to the kitchen I opened the fridge door and took three beers out.
Dave here's your beer, Darrell and here's yours.
We began talking by the time we had finished it was late morning. I began so
you are skin and you need some cash, let me help you Dave can you go to
my study and get my cheese book. Darrell's eyes opened wide he knew he
was on to something good.
"He will not be a minute".
"Fifty grand enough".

"His eyes widened more".

Yes. yes, thank you he said smiling.

But before I give you this you have to solely swear never to burgle again.

Oh right all right.

I could tell he was lying. Is that enough I handed him the calque.

That's more than enough he said snatching the money.

Thank you thank you mate. We sat there in the kitchen for a couple more hours after a hand full of beers and an

and an egg and bacon fry up I showed him the door.

I sparked up a cigarette a list of names flooded my head.

I had grown tired of all the meditation and I had also full filled my souls wishes. Everything was going well. The princess had a knew child who I dearly missed but I was very pleased. I was over the moon with my wife and her decisions and the things which had happened between me and her. For some reason I had no recollection of ever having sex with her which was a shame as I always thought about the intermesh of it.

But indeed all the signs were there when we met. I was at home but I had planned to make another visit to my new family. I was in the kitchen when I began to start thinking of everything that had happened there was a reason for everything. The thoughts were racing through my mind. Everything I thought was great but I was wrong. Something terrible was about to happen. I could hear screams coming from the other room. I sprinted across the kitchen down the corridor and into the lower bedroom what I could see was the cat it had attacked Eugene I could see this but Eugene could not.

She screamed out swinging at the air.

What the hell. She screamed

get out I shouted.

And what the hell are you doing in my bed room

pasty bloody creature she cried out.

I got close enough to thump it. But the cat was persistent.

He leaped of the bed and gave a grunt. Want some more do you. It screamed.

What is the problem cat? I shouted.

Who did you just speak to and who's the cat. Eugene asked.

I had to lie, diving on to the floor after the animal I was speaking to you cat is me knew nickname for you.

I tried shoving her through the bedroom door but she was persistent in wanting to walk back in this happened three times until I raised my voice would you please get out of this room?

I walked calmly to the window and opened it. Then I grabbed the pillow from my bed and unfolded it from its case. I waved it around the bedroom and tried to disguise the fact that we were being visited.

Eugene sued it straight away.

You can see something what what is it?

Before I had a chance to think of an answer Eugene said to me not to lie to her.

Nothing I can see nothing.

It was written all over my face. The cat I was told through my mind was trying to invite Eugene to visit them and to meditate with him.

I could read the cats mind like that.

It's no longer your secret the cat said pausing. We went for each other.

The cat laughed

Ha you missed.

What the hell what was that. Eugene cried out.

What was what. The cat was slowly dismantling my bedroom by throwing thinks at me and Eugene.

Then I got him.

Got you. I shouted.

The cat was now in the pillow case I rubbed the sweat from my forehead again and again and threw him out of the window and locked the window shut.

Eugene watched in amazement although there was nothing to see by her human eye

yet.

The cat strolled off as usual. I was going to be questioned I just knew it.

What the hell was that. Eugene said.

What was what That thing was it a ghost wait ok stop screwing with me.

I know something I mean that was something I said under my breath.

Okay okay.

That was …. there was a long pause

go on spill it I want the truth. Eugene said.

To be honest I cannot explain right now.

 Tell me she said corruptible and quickly with a shock in her voice.

I gulped and she gulped I went to leave the room but Eugene blocked the way by standing in the way of the door.

Tell me tell me please. She went on Is it a secret.

I cannot explain. I raised my voice. Now kindly step out of my way.

No. she stood there firmly in the door way in front of me.

Move I request it. I replied.

Not until you tell me what is going on.

I move closer to her suddenly the clouds in the sky started to move quickly day became night there was another storm brewing. The clouds were moving at a rapid speed something was wrong I could feel it. A storm had started. Suddenly there was a large bang lightning and thunder. It would have made your knees bend. One minute there was light the next minute total chaos in the sky and darkness.

The wind picked up fast, then it began to rain. Eugene was not thinking she went over to the window leaving the door unmanned then there was a large bang the thunder and lightning had hit the roof the electricity blew we were both in total darkness I managed to slip out of the room in to the darkened corridor.

That damn cat what was he trying to do. I said to myself.

I was not by the sea but it was early morning and I could see sea gulls they could talk a lot like cats but what they were talking about could open a massive scientific conversation. I was always thought that they were playing in some form or another. These particular gulls could speak human too just like cats.

I looked out the window I was upstairs in the spare room the main road a few houses were all I could see not much for a mute -million-pound estate bright lights shining down in a watery reflection of the road caught my eyes. I closed one eye and a tear fell from my face I was not upset a such it seemed or as it seemed I was a little upset about the cat I guess. Somehow I will have to explain to the others, going back to the birds they for some reason

they reminded me of bats I had not seen a bat for years maybe they had all died or something. I know they exist. Just before I had left the room upstairs I looked in the mirror I had grown even younger it was stupid and though it gave me a scare. I was glad I was the only person who could see this. But the pain did not leave it got worse and worse I looked down at my hands as I ran cold water on them it was soothing at the bedroom sink.

The swelling was immense they were feeling quite painful I started to cry tears ran down my face I needed to pull myself together I needed to meditate as I went to turn around I knocked a glass off the sinks side top it had smashed on the floor I quickly tidied it up I went down stairs and went to go into my room. The pain became so hard I passed out for a minute or two I was thinking about the cat. I sensed that something was wrong I got off my bed and sat in my chair crossed my legs and closed my eyes then that's when it happened the cat had got its claws out it was in my mind it jumped on me scratching my face and yelling at me I grappled with it pushing it onto the floor, my first instincts was to kick it but for some reason I went to pick up a pillow instead. It leaped at me, I took a swipe with the pillow, I missed just. Bloody hell, I said out loud.

The cat attack was nearly over I did not know why he was attacking me I did not know what I had done there was a short pause which gave me time to take the pillow out of its case I could use the case as a weapon.

Right you little get. I shouted as I raced towards it as it raced towards me it was going for my jugular I was told this time he missed stretching my arm.

You little bastard I shouted as I positioned myself for the next attack. It came at me again this time I swing a right hook and caught him in the jaw and winded it

my arm was stretched up bad by this time I took the pillow case again and dived at it across the room but I missed. It ran across the room and leaped out of the window into my garden I ran up to the window and closed it tightly.

What the hell I thought that cat is turning into a real handful I tidied the room up quickly luckily I did not make too much mess as before or too much noise. I opened and closed the window to make sure that the window was closed properly. I never thought the cat could be so devise it was like it had a spilt personally or something close. I needed a break I needed some rest bite I had to get away. It was not that I had enough money financially I was fine it was weather I could trust my house mates. I thought for this a while and in the end gave up. I walked to my study with a disgruntled look open my face. The cat gave me a real shock I had to ask myself if I should help him, weather he was telling the truth about wanting his real body back and how we were going to do it. To be honest I was not really bothered, why should I let the animal have a second chance, I was not going to get one so why should he. I climbed into bed pulling to bed covers over me. The window was open across the other side of the room and the fear was with in me. I was extremely tired and fell asleep quickly. This was the only time that I felt safe nothing could touch me as I was unconscious. Although I knew the morning was a hard thing to wake up to. and I had to admit that it was getting harder as time went by.

It was time for a change, there was many things which I had to take in to consideration stupid things, silly things such as what I was having for breakfast what I wearing, simple things like what aftershave I was using how many times away I would brush my teeth. I was also beginning to realize that my actions the things I did had consequences and affected other people. I could hear the sound of seagulls in the sky it was funny. It reminded me of the conversation we had last time we met. It was late there was a knock on the door I knew who it was it was Dave my cop. I greeted him with a smile he gave me a hand shake and a kiss and a hug. He was not surprised when I asked him where Eugene was he said properly at the club.
He struggled his shoulders and said leave me alone. He was drunk. What happened next was extremely saddening it broke my heart it was the cat a complained by the tramp who gave me the message the king whom we all dearly loved had other plans for my princess she was told never she had been told that we cannot meditate again and she was told that she must avoid all humans from now on. And our child was never to be mentioned on a human planet or plane again. Whatever happens now was going to be very costly. The cat and the tramp left my side. For some reason the cat had a big grin on its face I asked it why are you smiling in reply to this he just said nothing he just stared at me. That's when I clicked okay what have you done. The cat reply to this was to blow on his right paw then he rubbed his chest and said.
No shit.
then he continued.
Afterwards I had convinced myself that I should have one more journey the reason was that I had found time that I would find out was who the tramp really was. I was too tired to undress and wanted to get this over and done with walked through the large corridors of the mansion estate searching for the right room to meditate in even though I had thought of other rooms my room always seemed the right one so it was on. I did not strip. I pulled the glasses out of my pocket and took off my garments they were off me in seconds the journey had begun through the slip stream and out of my mind. As I traveling my mind went to different places and could see other people on the way who were doing the same. On the way I saw the cat and a little

further the president and off Couse the old tramp. I was focusing on the old tramp as he was the last person I saw but as I was travelling faster than light I did not have time to stop and speak to him and after all my experiences I still did not understand it fully the galaxy and the universes was an extremely big place. It was so vast that I do not think antibody really could understand it. As I was traveling past stars and through light I began to realize that the mind was an extremely beautiful in some places. Also I had

to answer a question to myself why was I trying to hide it for myself I guess it could be too dangerous and I did not want to put my house mates at risk. During this journey on which I was taking

chapter25 Oscar

something was not right I had meditated the across the through on to a different planet and as I had landed on it there was a loud crashing sound as if it was like a meteor had hit the suffice of which I was on. Everything had slowed down and It was like slow motion. I could not move my body and I could not bring myself back. All I could do is call upon assistants but there was none. Where was everybody after a minute or two I began to access my situation I felt for the very first time that I was in the wrong place. The suffice was quiet and there was nothing to see yet I did not like this, As I looked outwards and onwards my situation was not a good one. I began to way up the odds, well I said to myself If there was nobody here then I am safe except I did not feel safe and I knew that the feeling of being in danger very well. After around an hour or two of thinking and exploring the planet I decided I was going to make my way back. When I finally found the power to control my way back as it seemed like hours but infect it was only a few minutes. My whole body ached especially my head. I was so glad that I had made back it kind of taught me to be a little more careful in the future. I got off my bed I was sweating a fair bit I had not realized that I had not opened my eyes and when I did realize and tried I could not. At first I just thought they needed a wash so I got my eye wash out of the top of the cupboard and washed them but nothing I was not ready to panic Just yet. As I moved around my luxury bathroom knocking into things, trying to find something to hold on to. I stopped for a moment a pause to gather my thoughts, I tried desperately to force my eye lids up and back into my eyes. They were in there I could feel them. As an hour of persistent waiting I was about to give up I had been there counting the minutes into thoughts timing each time that I made an attempt to open them. I walked slowly out of the bathroom and into the bedroom clumsily knocking my shoulders and bumping into walls and plant pots just that little journey said it all I was blind. So I knew that my new situation was going to affect everything accept I also knew that it would not belong before I would be found. I took it rather easy only as I knew that my eyes would be restored I was relying on faith.

There was a knock on my bedroom door, I jumped with the shock of sitting there thinking. I did not really want to speak to anybody there was another knock slowly after. I really did not want to answer it. I got of the bed desperately trying to find some clothes. There was another knock I was busy trying to find some clothes all I could fine to wear was a T shirt I was semi naked so just as the door opened I just managed to jump into bed. I stuttered to speak as I was greeted.

Hay how are you.

Err there was a pause for a moment.

I'm fine what's up.

Were worried about you we have not heard from you for ages.

No I've been around here and there mostly at night.

I was making excuses but what you do not know does not hurt you. I could see at that point that I was about to be questioned.

Dave the guru was there also just standing by the door. I invited him in.

Come in Dave. I said loudly.

Dave shunted past the half open door.

Good to see you buddy what's happen in the world.

I wanted to tell them that I had partially lost my vision. To be honest it had not sunk in. they both started to bombard me with questions. They really must have missed me.

Okay I said and I insisted that I was fine neither of them noticed my eyes were shut, locked tight within my mind as for luck goes I had not removed the sun glasses. After an hour answering all there questions they finally began to leave. We discussed few things to do later on in the week and then at that point I was told that my movie was out so the money will come rolling in. I was kind of glad. But had I had other things on my mind. Then just as I thought that it was the end of the conversation Dave stuck his head around the corner of the door and told me that he had the tickets for the premier and it was tomorrow night. I replied with a thankyou but I knew I had to start getting used to being blind especially if I was going outside in public. So I asked myself what kind of things would a blind person try and teach himself if he could. I guess it was all about listening to sound and getting used to touching things and feeling things. Okay so I had forty-eight hours to understand me knew and latest problem. I began to walk about my bedroom touching things and bumping into things, I could feel my face when I felt my face I could feel the lines on my forehead of course it was me. I manage d to make my way to the wardrobe slowly rubbing the glass pained as I walked sideways to the end, then onto the window, then on to window ledge, knocking what I seemed to me to be a tube of hand cream on to the floor I picked it up. I put the lotion back only to knock other things over I bent down and tried to feel the floor for them again it was aftershave bottle then I knew it was because I could feel the top. I put the aftershave back on to the side. And picked up the tube of lotion slowly I squeezed the tube, and poured some of the lotion onto my hands I could smell it immediately. I think that I squeezed the tube a little bit too hard as my prams was filled with cream. I walked to the bathroom with my arms out dripping the cream off my hands onto the floor I walking towards my bed it was in front me bumped into my bed I knew I was going in the wrong direction now so I turned around it was harder than you think. I was finally going in the right direction. This time I tried to walk there without my arms as an aid and decided to count my steps. I could smell some the lotion into my hands I could smell it immediately. It was like everything in my body had changed obviously my eyes then my senses all of them my nose and defiantly my ears. I did not have to think about them I could hear everything from the TV to the traffic to the birds in the trees. I got to the bathroom and felt one side of the room I found what I was looking straight away it was a towel. I wiped the hand cream off and put the towel back. On coming out of the bathroom and going back to my bedroom I continued to look for things to touch and feel. Then suddenly the pain hit me, it was like tokening a bullet, first of all the most the excruciating pain hit my mouth ten or even twenty times more painful than a tooth ache, then the chest again it was far worse than a heart attack. The pain ripped through my upper body forcing me to the ground onto my knees. With one arm out I fell from my knees onto my side trying to fight the pain I was going to pass out, I could not shout as it would startle the other, I needed a sound proof room quickly I needed a stick to bite on the pain was bearable, I was being taken to my limits but I did not want to lose I tried my hardest to pull myself together. I managed to get back on my knees the only thing I needed was a pain killer. I crawled into my bathroom blind it was like I was never going to make it to my medicine cabinet. One I could not see and other was the pain I was in was incredible. I had to get up off my feet, the first time I failed smashing my face not hard but hard enough to wind myself more pain I thought I had broken my jaw. I reached up to the cabinet with one hand pushing all of the medicine out of the cabinet onto the floor their some of the jars were broken. I was struggling but still I did not cry out. Just as I going to give up a tube rolled to my feet I scampered in a hurry to feel what I found. I could tell by the shape of the jar by its feel that it was the pain killer, I was in so much pain I opened the jar in a hurry and did not bother about the water until afterwards. A few minutes later the pain was gone I counted the pain killers just in case I need end them for later.

As I finally became to be more normal even though I could not see at this point the pain had receded I was stubbing around one for being out of pain the other reason was that I must have been tired and I could not see. As I moved around the bedroom the thought of wanting to touch things had aspired. All I wanted to do was to get back into bed, As I climbed in I felt the warmth of the bedding but I could see nothing. I pulled the covers over me I was in total darkness. I just wanted to sleep I could not be bothered about the award ceremony, although it was important that I had to teach myself how to be normal and not blind so people would not know. I was laying there hugging my pillow close to my face trying to find a way, I was thinking real hard almost every second was another thought an idea of how I was going to beat this or not. The water in my mouth was building up. This was worse than meditation all in all the thought of meditating did not reach me infect I did not think at the time to meditate and try and find another answer to put me at peace. I

closed my eyes even though I did not want to go to sleep because
of the timing of the award ceremony the pressure in my mind was too much I had to sleep. I set my alarm clock for a few hours and I slept for a couple of hours hoping that my vision would come back. But it had not I through the bedding off me kind childlike, and paused at the edge of it. I rubbed my face I could feel its shape. There had to be an answer nobody just goes blind I was

thinking and thinking and thinking for hours but nothing I was waking up the odds the whys the when and the how. Then I came across the conclusion that it had something to do with my last meditating journey to the unnamed planet. It was that journey that I took which was the problem and the answer was that I had to go back there but I did not have time. What was I going to do now and I was pretty confident that I had found an answer? I Withheld the thought within myself. And I had decided that I was going to the awards blind. Never the less I had to practice I could do this I was an actor after all. I knew where I was while I sat there on my bed the problem was that I did not know if I had enough time to pull it off. It was certainly a completely different feeling and sensation I wanted to go outside for a walk but first I had to get dressed. I stood up and almost fainted I guess it was light headedness. To start with my whole body felt weak especially my legs. I could not visualize anything and I wanted to see my wardrobe but there was nothing. I had to find things by my memory which seemed easy enough. As I walked across the bedroom calmly and taking each step with precaution, moving slowly I began to move towards the wardrobe I was approaching the door. The first thing I did was to stretch out my arms to touch it. Eventually I found the door knob and opened the wardrobe door, I reached in and pulled out what was a shirt and I felt a little higher on the shelves for a pair of jeans. I took the garments back across the room laying them on my bed. The next task was to find myself a vest and some socks after I had done this I began to dress. The clothes felt soft as I put them on It is funny that all the times that I had dressed myself at this point I had realized that so many take the little things for granted. I was nearly dressed all I needed was my shoes. I got onto my feet and headed towards the wardrobe again it was not getting any easier, there was a pain in my foot and it had gone numb, I kind of began to limp I needed to sit down and have a stretch. After a couple of minutes, the feeling in my foot and toes had receded and I was able to go on my way back to the wardrobe, When I got there

I felt for a pair of shoes which were on a shoe rack just inside the wardrobe doors I picked up a pair after sorting through for a minute or two. I walked back to my bed feeling the bed before I sat down upon it. after I had finished dressing I played back on my bed sitting up with my pillows piled high behind my back. I could not meditate as I could not see and I wanted my vision back. I did not expect it at this time and I was never one for tears but this time was my situation was really beginning to get me up set. I could not cry it was not in my nature. I'm the kind of fellow who would just bottle everything up. Because it did not like weakness although in saying that I'm not saying that crying at this moment in time would properly help me. As I said this to myself. I was thinking of how I would get myself out of the situation and try to get used to the pitch black darkness that I was now in. It was getting late and I was slowly running out of time. I wanted to study everything through touching things There was plenty of thinks in my bedroom to do so. It was not easy gathering things around my bedroom anything and everything, from bedding to aftershave bottles to toilet paper, shoes and other clothes. Then there was the walking it was extremely difficult. After a minute or two I Knew that I could not walk without an aid, so I walked to my wardrobes to see if I had a walking stick in fact when I got there and had a good feel I found four. That was better it was a lot easier and in just that took the some of the pressure off me. It did not take me long to get used to being blind even though I could not see but I could feel and smell it was like a senses over load. I had become extremely sensitive. I could smell the fresh air and the clothes and the wooden floor boards. I had one more day to memories movement and feeling so I continued grabbing things and touching items and walking. After all of this what worried me the most was how was I going to find my way back and even more so how was I going to tell the others the guru David and Eugene, if I told the cat and the president I'm not sure that they would understand. I was finally getting used to my new condition and I was thinking hard how I was going to pull it off.

After another day of touching and feeling things and objects I began to memorized the things that I felt.

It was in the morning of the very special night that began to feel more unsure of what I was going to do. I really did not want to miss the awards but as I thought about more the more uncertain that I became. my mind was closed I made sure of that, and I was on the edge of my bed in excitement. I had finished in the bedroom and wanted to venture out. I had been in the bedroom for a long time as I tried to recall the time it must have been a good three months. I had already had the sunglasses on so there was not much point in taking them off as I needed to hide my eyes from everybody. I could remember were the kitchen was and I wanted to take the journey for the experience if anything. I did not know if there was anybody in the mansion with me and if there was I'm sure that I would be quiet enough to make it to the kitchen. I unlocked the door which was controlled electrically. It was a basic alarm, and was efficient for its's needs. So I was in the corridor trying to walk in a straight line it was quite hard, as I walked I found myself bumping into the hallway walls. Occasionally bumping into the sides of the walls, knocking the odd picture off here and there. The first was the Mona and then the Picasso I knew this by their size and shape, Setting the alarms off. This gave me the notion that my house mates were out as nobody came into the great hallway to see what was the bother. The noise was loud but as there was nobody around I could take my time putting them back.

I looked inside my pocket for a smoke all I could find was a butt, it did not bother me as all I wanted was a puff smoking can be so addictive. As I came to the end of the hall way and entered the kitchen there was lots of things I could play with, you know things I could touch and feel. Although in reality thinking about the awards all I really had to do was to walk about twenty meters and stand there and walk back to my seat it was simple as that. I pulled up a seat and began to think about it. What I was scared about was the walk I could only imagine that if I was up for any of the awards I was going to have to walk depending on where I was sitting. I was not whether I would be at the back of the theater or at the front. Either way it was not going to be easy.

I tried to go about the day as normal as possible but the emotions started stirring in.
one second I was happy the next I was sad. Why I had this horrendous occurrence had happened to me. All I knew that that journey to the other planet had left me blind and the only answer was that I had was that I had some of the planets dust in my eyes. I know it sounds crazy but it was the only other theory that I had. While I had been thinking of this I was not able to continue with the meditation.

A few more hours, eighteen to be exact and I would be off to the awards I was excited, And the thought was all there all about winning. As I sat there on the edge of my bed I was slowly falling asleep and a few minutes later managed to pull Myself to gather after an hour I wanted to know the time and I was a little reluctant to go find my house mates as I was still trying to hide the fact that I was blind. I picked up my walking stick and walked out of the bedroom I was confident that I could pull the act off that's all it was for me. It was quite confident that I was doing it. as I walked out of the bedroom and went right instead of left towards the lounge. I felt around for my arm chair I was feeling a little bit clever as I found my chair first time. All I had to do was to wait for my house mates. Going back, I wanted to know what the time was. So before I sat down I walked towards the wall, I already knew where the big clock was. It stood about two feet above the fire place and I also knew that it was the clock face was written in roman numerals. I felt up to the clock and touched its hands. I now had the time. I was relived and I sat down my favorite chair. It was totally quiet there was not a sound or even a bird in the sky not that I could see them but I could hear. suddenly a gust of wind blew straight in. Somebody had left the window open and there was some thunder there was going to be a storm. I stood up thinking carefully how I was going approach the swinging windows in the storm as they were crashing violently together but now I was sticking out me

walking sticks franticly to feel the windows. I caught the first one on the right pushing it hard with the walking stick. To close it. It shut immediately then I was not going to try and lock it until I

chapter26 Rain storm

had caught the other one, then suddenly there was a great gust of wind it blew the window door right open then shut them was silent again. I walked up to the doors and locked them both. With great relief I sat down again and waited for the others arrive. That is when I realized that I had to get dressed I got up again for the affiant time well you know what they say no rest no play. Being kind of angry with myself back to my bedroom.

I opened the door slowly and walked in clumsily slightly stumbling like a drunk. I was just putting the walking stick down on the bed to make my way to the wardrobe. I was really trying my hardest in choosing the right clothes. I knew what the clothes looked like in my mind from previous experiences I was feeling for techier I just did not know yet were the suit was. I was Looking, feeling each suit jacket. I was lucky in feeling for the tuxedo as it was slightly a different material from my other suits. Which made it a little bit easier to find. After a few minutes I found what I thought was the tux.

Then I made it back to my bed and started to undress. It was not particularly hard it was just getting use to remembering where things were. Just as I was finishing there was a knock on my door I sat there on the bed and spoke out gently. Then the door opened it was Eugene and the guru David. They were shouting out with excitement jumping on me and rushing me out of the room down the corridor to the front door.

"Look she said we have got a limo".

I did not reply.

"Go on get in". Eugene said in like a childish manner bumping past me opening the door.

I stepped forwards I could not see a thing; I was guessing that as it was a limo we would all be sitting in the back. I was thinking that this was a test a half. I moved a bit closer. In my mind I could feel its presents. I decided to leave it in Gods hand's and made a guess and again I was right. The limo's door was exactly where I predicted. I put my hands on the roof and ducked in. As we were close to town the journey was not going to be too long. I still felt quite nervous and on top of that I was properly up for an award. In fact, I knew I was, it was a little bit obvious as I always knew when David was handing things because he would give off certain vibes. Like he would start cracking jokes which were not even funny and then he would laugh at them and he would laugh at nothing then say it was nothing he was just thinking. As the journey came to an end It was time to start worrying again there was cheers everywhere and I knew that I could not afford to wait around for the press. Unlucky for me at this time. As I made my way into the theatre I bumped straight into a couple of camera men. The cheers were mind blowing. As I helped them both to their feet as I knocked them both over with the urge to get inside and hide out of people's way. They followed me into the theatre. I stopped as I gave in, I felt the camera power and I did not walk off again until the clicking of the machines dispensed into the outside of the building. Now that I was on my own I had a chance to calm down and coolly took a cigarette out of my packet, I held it in my mouth for a moment and lit it up, as there was nowhere to ash I wounded of to find the gentlemen's toilet, when I got there I walked in this gave me a chance to grab some composure. I had the sinks that meant the toilets were behind me that's when I turned around and walked in. pushing the door open. I sat down on the toilet the seat was up already I planted my bottom on it and finished off my cigarette slowly aching the end into the toilet. just as I had I finish there was a voice and a knock at the toilet door.

and then the person called out.

"Are you alright sir".

I answered.

"There is a no smoking policy here in this hotel".

I got off the seat and pushed the toilet door open an answered him while I was pulling my wallet out of my tux from the inside pocket. Holding out in my hand a couple of fivers, and quickly apologizing. I pushed the fivers into his hand. He stepped aside and bumped pass him and walked out shutting the door behind myself and leaving the servant behind. As I walked through the corridors back to the main lobby there were people everywhere I did not have to see the people as the sound of the crowd cheering and chanting was incredible. At that point I wished I could see. I walked around using my walking stick to guide me, at this time I thought a good drink would help or not. I could hear everything it was like I had lost my eyes and gained hearing. I was just about to give in and find a seat to rest in for the moment but as I did I bumped sleight into a small girl good teenager she was holding a boxes of popcorn. It was something that was related to cinema for years and years. Fortunately, I did not bump her hard enough to knock the popcorn over and out of her hand 'and off the tray. I told that I was sorry and she excepted the apology. I did not ask her name and she was confident enough to ask me if I wanted a bucket of popcorn.

"How much ".

She replied "small box three pounds". She continued.

"Large box three fifty

I did not hesitate to pull a couple of hundred pounds out of my pocket although as I could not see I struggled to count it out I knew how much I was counting as I could feel the money. It was textured each picture and style and the size. I was feeling generous and just gave her the Ten-pound note. She handed me the popcorn and When I took it from her I told her to keep the change.

She thanked me and I moved into the rest of the crowed. I believed that I was now going up stairs into the actual theatre I was keeping cool. But it was enterable that I was going to Take a fall luckily it was not backwards but forwards. The actors behind me caught me as I fell forwards. I hit the floor still slipping forwards and quickly got back on to my feet. As the crowd came to a standstill and for a moment client then within a few seconds a few cheers, I calmly got back onto my feet and as I did I felt a godly pull I knew who it was it was Dave the guru and Eugene. They greeted me with greatness, Eugene was drunk and the guru was just complimenting me with gestures such as you fifth rich get, I have not met so many people in my life. Do you know who I have just been speaking too. At that point I just laugh and put one hand up onto the right shoulder to steady myself. I wanted to take the sun glasses off and reveal myself I wanted to share the truth. It was a fight within me maybe it was not the right place although the publicity would be good. As the thought of disguising myself and telling them the truth was there. Dave asked me if I was listening to him Yeah who

"You would not believe this". He continued with a list of talent.

I was miles away trying to stay focused around the stars and celebrity's I was beginning to break with the pressure, I asked Dave to take us to our seats and he did. I still sure that he did not notice my problem. And I was not sure whether he would catch on but I had to ask him a couple of questions in case I was called to the stage, yes I was that high profile. I was lucky that he was drunk and did not take me to seriously when I bombed him with question about where we were sitting, how mint steps do you think it would take from our seats to the stage. The ceremony went on for hour's actor after actor ward after award, I was quite surprised that I had not been called to go up to the stage. I asked Dave for the time he gave it to me it could not be long now I was getting sweaty and a little bit anxious with show I needed a cigarette I lent sideways onto arm of the chair I called him a couple of times he was asleep. I gave him a nudge and woke him him. I asked him for a cigarette he told me he did not have any but he had a cigar. I whisper to him could I have it, he obliged and passed it to me.

As I was smoking it, the Actor on stage was just opening the final envelope I waited there was a pause then actor said her name I did not believe it in fact I kind of lost my temper and I had lost the nomination for the ward too the tears swelled up in my eyes and Dave held my me squeezing my arm harder and harder. I told Dave to let go but he did not until I shouted the worst words at him. I'm glad the actors who were around me at that time took no notice. He then let go.

We left the venue in style we left in the limo, I was kind of sadden by the company that within the last few years that my work was not good enough. I went into deep conversation with adze about this and It did not stop until the limo stopped outside the mansion. I was in a sad amazement whatever that means. Dave payed the drive who seemed to be kind of pleased with his

work for the evening. I had already got out of the limo and started heading for the door Then I realized that we had forgotten
chapter27 going nowhere

Eugene I turned around and got back into the limo. Dave was drunk and was not particularly bothered. I told him to wait he was just about to step on the pavement when he realized.
Oh dear he said we have seemed to have forgot Eugene. I knew he knew. I finally convinced
him that we should go back and find her. We both got back into the limo and told the driver to go back. As we were being driven back to the venue we discussed if she would be there. She was not the kind of person who would just walk off. I told the driver to put his foot down as I was tired and Dave was drunk. I started to talk about her and I was saying to Dave that really she was old enough and ugly enough to look after herself. I knew that the journey was not long, I picked up my mobile phone and dialed her mobile. Just as we were pulling over at the venue I could see her, she was alone and she looked too drunk to be upset she was busy trying to answer her phone, as I had just called her. the limo pulled up next to her. She was as drunk as a skunk, she was holding the mobile phone in one hand and a bottle of wine in the other.
"where have you been"
"We forgot you and that's the truth."
 Eugene got in the limo.
"I know you lost, so did I."
She closed her eyes for a moment. Then she said "we will get them next time were a team", and then she started to cry.
I said nothing I had more to think about like how I was going to get my eyes back. even more so how I was going to tell the both of them that I was blind.

When I had got inside the mansion I walked straight to my room unaided as I had left my walking stick in the limo. I properly will not see it again, Dave was closely behind me he called out good night and pushed past me on the

92

way to the kitchen properly going for a coffee, Eugene was close behind him and she pushed on the back to as I was just walking in to my room. I called back agreeing though I knew I could be locked away for a long time behind my bedroom door. Good night Eugene had a smile on her face again which was normal for her.

I had decided to undress on the top of my bed removing the clothes was easy, it was finding something to wear which was not going to be so easy. I typed in the security number on its panel to resume that nobody could get in it made a bleeping sound as you pushed the buttons.

then a long buzz when it was locked. And sat on my bed I was telling myself that I was going to be okay I had more questions. However, I was reasonably tired and just wanted to sleep The thought of just sleeping was daunting and I was worried until I began to settle. As I did more and more ideas came into mind I could not see them but I could feel them it was all going to be a new experience for me or maybe it was a new adventure.

When I awoke I thought it was early morning but in fact it was late afternoon I knew this by because of the feeling of the day and the consistent of the air in my room. I got out of bed the right way leaving one blanket on the bed and the other half on the bed and half on the floor. then I tried to open my eyes nothing, I was disappointed and continued to the window to open it to let the light in not that it made any difference now. I was really missing the experience of the meditation and I was not going to give up in finding my vision again. Standing by the window was going to be my place for a while. I was think about the good times and did not realize that they were actually really good times and in a way I had taken them for granted. I continued their had to be away to bring me back as most things have an end and a beginning, I stood there for a couple of more minutes than the word reverses me came in to my mind. Something felt right about those words as I thought about them more and more I began to feel a lot better. I had found an answer the tears began to

surge from me and as they did they filled my closed eyes cleaning the red dust from the planet out onto my bedroom floor as I was being restored the red dust poured from my eyes. The power of the dust forced me backwards knocking me onto the floor I was trying desperately to pick myself up. I rolled off my back then on to one knee but the dust forced me back on to my back although this only lasted a few minutes it felt like a life time. I was really fighting for my eyes, eventually the planet gave in the dust had departed up and out of the window. I could see clearly now. Where it went I do not know.

It was only there for a few seconds as it left there was a ghostly whistle to the sound of its movement as it rose up in like a twister and disappeared outside through my bedroom window.

After I had my eyes restored and I could now see again I was amazement I started by looking at my arms, then my legs, and then the inside of my mouth. There was a simple sensation running through my body it was like a tingling feeling from head to toes. Inside I was totally at ease and at one in myself and at peace. I could see again. I need to get some breakfast so I took a stroll to my kitchen where my chief was we greeted each other with a smile and I patted on the shoulder continuing the greeting. I told him what I wanted and asked him to take it to my room, and I would be their shortly. I was walking around the house when I remembered some of the experience that I had, and wondered when my mind would contact my old friends in the spiritual world. They were properly thinking the same. I came to the conclusion that it was too early to make a journey as I wanted more time to heal.

The time seemed to fly by one minute it was noon, mid-day the next second it was night. and I was looking at the moon at this point and it seemed to be a lot closer than usual, any way I was not a scientist and maybe it was just the way I was seeing things at the moment. As the night went on I was extremely happy with the day's recurrences although I wanted to sleep I was hesitant on what I was going to see when I closed my eyes. In the end I was just sitting there on my bed and slowly falling in and out of consciousness and then finally I fell asleep. It was early

in the night when I awoke, there was not anything that disturbed me. As I was waking up I had a stretch and a yawn Normally I would wake up in cold sweats or hearing thinks even more so halogenation. There was nothing.

None of these occurred and it kept me puzzled or a minute or two. I was trying to figure out where everybody had gone that's when the paranoia set in I started to ask myself questions on top of questions. I let of my bed trying to suck an answer from my mind. It was easy I was losing my mind, I was trying to calculate everything. things like all how's and whys the when's and the what's something said to me that I had been in this kind of mood before.

That's when it started again. I was getting hot again and I had begun sweating I rushed to the bathroom ripping the t- shirt off and throwing it onto the floor, by the time I had got there I had stripped naked. I looked in the mirror my face was red and the sweat poured from my head on to my body which was already boiling hot. I was at the bathroom sink and turned the cold tap on as the water flowed out I began splashing it over my body, until I cooled down however it was not working as soon a washed the first lot of sweat off the next lot of sweat began and I was not getting any cooler. I grabbed a towel from the rail rack and rapped it around my head and face. By the time I had made it to my bed the first visitor had arrived It was the seagull. It was a larger bird than I imagined and I knew that his boss only sent him to me to annoy me. It began by pecking the window it was like a vampire I could hear its squeaking voice. It was not going to leave until I had let it in. The bird was defiantly crazy, it was at my window flapping its wings and twisting while pecking the air. I opened the window and gave him a push a hard push as to usher it away, and told it to go away, I have to agree it was extremely persistent. If you could see it you would have laugh, this was serious.

I was slowly getting more and more paranoid I was sitting there thinking about nothing for a while then in a sudden rush all I could think about was having my sight back at the moment. But it was soon to change the paranoia set in and it set in fast. Everything that I looked at seemed to look back at me, and every thought that I thought about attacked my mind it was extremely painful especially when I thought of people. This feeling was from above and I kind of knew this so we were even I guess. The night went on I did not believe that it would ever stop it was that powerful to the mind even the night played as the sky's clouds g

altered into a rain storm. I was beginning to think that I wanted
                    chapter28 Deep talking

out. I was thinking about my child I miss him quite a lot, he must be a least seven by now. I was not sure whether I should try and contact him as there were certain rules. It had been a long time since I had been on that plane. I suppose that you could call it his realm. I could imagine him sitting there he was obviously going to be powerful. Thinking of my son only encouraged me to think about my wife the princess, I was thinking about what she said she said something about that she would contact me rather than me sucking for her. I was kind of disappointed with that agreement but she was the princess and she was normally right.

I continued pacing around my bedroom occasionally looking out of my bedroom window watching the storm. There was thunder and lighting and it was getting worse and worse.

For the first time in about a few years I was feeling nice and calm. That's when I realized that I had forgot to look at the mirror, I was a little scared it was a weird feeling that came over me and as I knew that whatever I was going to see was going to ruin my day and properly my mood. I did not want to think about it too much and I was slowly getting more and more harder to decide. I think this was a test of some sort a test of faith, As I thought of it more after thinking about the word faith It hit me quite fast. I removed myself from the window and paced to the bathroom. I did not hesitate to look into the mirror. What I saw startled me the image of myself. I took a deep breath and turned away. How could this be the letter was right. I approached the mirror once more, in that mirror I saw a child it must have been about two. The letter was right, as I must recall how I was could turn myself back. and also I was pretty happy that only I could see

this but I had to remember. As for this moment in time I was lost for answers in fact my mind which was usually full of ideas was now empty. It did not matter how many time s I thought of it the thought it was lost. This was quite upsetting and it put me in a mood. As for that I was reasonably feeling okay. I closed my eye s and it became quite a shock there was a girl in my mind. I wondered what that strange feeling was I her what her name was. I ready knew that she was friendly as she was a dark red in color.

I did not want another conversation at the moment as my eye were still healing but the girl was persistent and so was I. That's when she told me that she came to give me an apology from her planet. I was raised up over the conversation what planet I asked forgetting that I been blinded by her. There was silent for a minute between us then I caught on the red planet. With that she left and that was that she did not even blink she just disappeared. She seemed like a nice lady and thinking back of what she said made me smile. I continued to pace around my bedroom, there was always a strange feeling about my place now it was a good feeling it was a kind of welcoming feeling a kind of feeling that anything could exists in the room. I had fallen in love with mansion it was a great, each room had its significant. The drawing room and my bed room, the living room and the kitchen and there was more upstairs. The best thing about the mansion was its hall ways and its large curtains, which I used to play around with when I was a child. Thinking about the past kind of bought a kind of sadness to me the laughter had worn off and all that was left was sadness. I wanted to go for a walk as I missed the mansion I could hear David in the back ground as I secretly crept out into corridor and the noise of the TV, and went for a stroll. I did not know how much I had missed the place everything was in place each and every pitcher and ornament. Dave the guru and Eugene had keep the place emasculate, obviously with some help from the cleaners. I walked around for an hour going to room to room pulling faces and having a joke as I went by. Most of the rooms were guest rooms and were not in use. Although I have had some rich people visit me. As I walking I could hear a chiming I knew what it was straight away. That was my grandfather clock that had been there for around forty years. I did not want to go to it as it was just finishing it chimes, it echoed through the corridors and then suddenly it stopped. I was in one of the guest rooms I was in the position to stick my head around the corner of the door and I did so. I was expecting to see a ghost or something like in the movies after the spooky clock chiming, you know like the ghost of the last owner or even worse the ghost of the maid or something along those lines. I continued my walk until I came to a room that was locked I gave it large push and twisted the dark half painted handle, the door was shut tight. Although I knew that I could use a key if I Could find it on my key ring so I began to such for my key ring which I when I go walking around always carry.

Even though none of the keys fitted the lock I really wanted to kick the door down just to see what was in there. But my mind got the better of me and I decided to revisit the room at another time. I found that discovery rather exciting. I already knew that we were ghost free but I could imagine an old piano and the ghost of the mansion sitting there playing it. the thought again made me smile after I had finished my tour on my own. I made my way back down to my hall way I checked the post there was nothing in there for me. I could still hear the guru David watching the TV. As I was just going to pass the kitchen my chef came out he was carrying some food on a tray I could see clearly that for that moment what was going to occur as he came out of the kitchen holding the tray with one hand he was going to bump right into me but cleverly he had the tray held high and I managed to avoid it by spinning myself under his arm and then around his body. He did not reptile he just kept on walking and that was a near miss. It was like a movie stunt, something you would see on TV.

I wanted a drink so I continued into the kitchen as I was by it. there were all sorts going on in here. pots and pans everywhere. Whatever he was cooking smelt good. I opened the fridge door and took a couple of bottles of beer out. Just as I did the chef walked back in. He said nothing. I said cheers swinging my body out of his way. I made my way back down the corridor. For some reason I did not want to drink alone but I did not want to disturb the guru Dave as I could clearly see that he was busy watching TV and he was properly in his element.

I found a place where I could relax and it was back into my study as I walked in the atmosphere of the old room filled the air. I found my place to think and drink. I pulled up a seat and sat down opening the both of the bottle feeling the chill of the bottles on the palms of my hands. Slowly taking a swig of the beer, there was a cool sensation as the cold fluid hit the back of my throat. It was a pleasant feeling. I shuffled forwards reaching into my pocket for a cigarettes and I was lucky enough to find a couple, I pulled one out and lit it up. Again the smooth sensation reaches me like a hit and it was a hit that I was taking it felt cool.

I drank my beers slowly one after another, it did not take me much to get drunk now a day. As I finished the second bottle I passed out only to be woken a few minutes later it seemed like a life time. I did not want to leave this room as there seemed to be a certain atmosphere in here. I asked him where he was going he replied with a polite vocal home. I then asked him why.
and if he had been offered a room his reply was no. well I said there is room he for you and you can stay there in it for free whenever you like as you

work for me.

The chef's eyes lit up he thanked me and said he will see me tomorrow. My reply was no worry's I had to shout it out quickly as he was just going through the door.

That made me feel good not that I was not feeling good in the first place I was really quiet fine. I looked forwards to actually meeting him. I finally got into my room and parched myself in a chair. I turned the lights off and watched my window, the curtains where open and the darkness fell in. I was expecting an animal I was guessing that it would be the crazy cat or an even crazier seagull. I waited and waited but nothing. I knew what I was waiting for and they were keeping me waiting. I knew that they knew that I knew that they were going to wait until the early hours of the morning to call on me knowing that I would be more unable as I had no sleep. It was early in the mooring I could have not felt any worse. My eyes were half closed and I was feeling sick not sick as poorly but the feeling sickness of wanting to sleep it was the feeling of paranoia and lack of sleep. I was fighting it was not going to beat me. I went to the window in such for some fresh air as I opened it they were there.

"We have been watching you and waiting".

"yeah yeah".

"There are not coming to visit you will have to find them yourself".

I thought about what the sea gull was saying and he was being backed up by the crazy cat.

I did not speak I was miles away trying to figure out what the hell was a sea gull all about.

"who was he". I asked it was otiosely the reincarnation of someone

The cat replied "I cannot tell you that".

then he cheekily said. "Figure it out for yourself ".

I said fine. Then he said fine and politely asked if he could come in. I thought about it for a minute and stupidly let them in. So what's in the world of meditation I asked him there was silence at first then he told me. That more and more people were following him, and it was him that had blinded me and the visit that I had from the red lady was him also. I told that he was lying which this cat did often. I told him my feelings but he proved me wrong by closing his eyes and changing himself into the red lady I could not believe it so I said how did and why did I go blind that was the tramp you see he sprinkle some of the red planets dust on you as you were meditating by him he w s extremely dangerous.

"I shall go on "

"No no please do not I have heard enough".

"But please".

"I said close it big mouth".

"Then the cat joined in" and I also know that you are now a big baby see, they were speaking to me in cantor and sustainably "It was all us and you did not even smell a rat it just goes to show you does it not Just how thick humans are meek and weak".

Okay I agreed just to shut them up. I asked them if they had heard anything from my wife they said they had not. I did not believe them. the bird or the cat. I went to pick up the cat and it let me so I said while stroked the cat what else have you been up to, the sea gull was gear to answer the snapped at it and told it to shut its beak. I reentered the conversation answering as nicely in a calm voice not that it made any difference. Its beak was now firmly shut. I tried again this time stroking the cat a little harder, come on I said you can tell me.

the cat again said keep quiet.

Come on then cat let's see how clever you really are the cat was perch on my Knee I took my hands off it as it refused to answer please please show me something. It knew something again I spoke out show me. The cat showed me nothing. In a way that was properly the best. I could properly teach my self exactly what the cat knew in saying that I do not know what to think about a crazy seagull. I told the pair of them that I was tired and wanted them both to leave. I threw them both out closing the window behind me and drawing the curtains. In a way I was disappointed that my child never contacted me on that night, maybe he was still too young and relishing now that it might take a decade, but I was sure that my princess would have told him and taught him for the love for me. I laid on my bed it was warm enough just to lay on top of bed. after all the excitement and the visit from the two crazy animals the cat and the bird I was left to think about whether I should sleep as it was reasonably early in the morning. I leant over onto my side a reached out for my alarm clock which was on my bedroom side table. I lent a little too much and knocked it onto the floor. It was one of those old fashioned alarm clocks with the old fashioned bells on top you have to wind it up whenever you use it hit the floor hard and the sound of the bell rang out not enough to wake anybody in another room but just enough to wake me up as I was half asleep and just going back to bed. I was now awake. It was early morning. I needed a cup of coffee and some breakfast my chef was not in just yet and like usual the fridge and cupboards had been raided all that was left was a bag of popcorn and half a jar of coffee. I stretched out arm into the cupboard and grabbed the jar and put it on the kitchen side board it did not look to appetizing. I opened the lid, luckily the granules were soft. I was even more surprised when I opened the popcorn it was in date and still edible. I made my self the coffee first then I opened the packet of popcorn while listening to the kettle then I started to eat the popcorn. It was not the the right food to be eating in the morning but it was all I had. I was normally quite serious about what I consumed at what time of day. But popcorn would do for now I was not feeling fussy. The dry taste of the popcorn was not particularly nice at first I was eating it fast and washing it back with a swig of the coffee. I had never felt any better and I was enjoying being me again. As I moved around in the kitchen like I was dancing I heard a voice as clear as the day it was just in front of me and to the side. I dropped the cup smashing it on the floor. I swear at the incident. I left the kitchen worrying and I walked in a hurry to get back to my room. When I walked in I was in shock they were back. I could not see them though it was not that I was blind because I was not and I had not asked the them the question why I could not see them but I could hear them. I asked them what they wanted there was no answer. I ask them if they had a message for me and again no answer. I could feel them touching my face they were as soft as a feather they were reasonably friendly. As I sat down on my bed a tingling feeling began in my face and it raced right down to my feet I was incredible feeling my legs went numb and it was pleasurable pain it was filling me with love. This feeling lasted for a short while five may ten minutes and it put me in a better mood although I was already in a reasonably good mood I was laughing up to the point that I had begun to weep a little. The tear ran down my face and fell on to the floor. I did not notice it after that but something strange happened as soon as the tear hit the floor it began to expand it started off as a tear drop then within a few second s it had become a puddle and within sixty second s it had covered most of the floor. The tear was getting bigger and bigger extremely fast. before I had a chance to let myself out it was at knee height. I waded through the giant tear puddle to my bedroom door and tapped in the alarm security number it did not work. The tear was getting even bigger it had reached my waist line I was not happy, I continued to push the alarm panel. I had to

get out of the room or open the bedroom door to let the water out. It took me a few more moments and brute strength the door opened slowly and the tears persisted out. Nothing in the room was wet. But that was not the end as I walked over to my bed I could feel that there was something wrong in my mind. It seemed to be heavy and I could hear a trembling sound like a thunder storm no it was like a waterfall. Second s later it happened again it but this time it was from my eyes it started off slowly just a tear then it got more persistent until my eye s was totally filled that's where the problem was they became over filled the water flooded from my eye s. forcing backwards onto the floor I raised my hand s to my head in order to support head more. The water was getting more furious as it poured out of my eyes but as I took more control of it I was able to control it away I did not know how I knew how to do I just did. Only this time there was damage all my things were broken or were soaked threw. I had to ask myself what was that, what did I just experience. I checked my eyes to see what was the damage was to my surprise there was none.

I could not tidy my room myself as it was not in my nature so I just left it as it was I would have to wait for my cleaner they normally come on a Sunday, with the window cleaners.

I sat there in a mess and did not really know what to do I was staring around my room in a kind of dream state, not that it made any difference as I had already lost my mind. I did not notice at first but my clothes were actually soaked through and I had to change them. But before I did I decided to take a stroll in my garden there was not so much to see. Eugene had turned it into her playground and I was wondering how she was there was a note on the fridge I knew that I had read it. She was in France for a week on the cat walk and then she wrote she was going to France for a break she was always traveling and properly had seen most world. I walked father up the garden the I could feel her presents she was a stronger one that's when I found it. I was surprised when I found it, at the very top of my garden there was a small patch of grass neatly cut. It looked to me to be a place of meditation. It sucked me into it, the power was incredible. there was a large circle then another circle inside of that and so on continuous. It seemed strange but I had to try it but I was going to wait until the evening. In a way that was kind of wrong as you would think that I would think that I would prefer the light but as for this moment I was enjoying the darkness not saying that there's something wrong about the light but it's a bit powerful and you could feel it. I walked back to the big glass patio doors and slid in.

The thought of the grass circles made me smile again and again and thought of the grass circles was amazing. I waited at the bus stop for the bus it only took a few minutes before people started turning up. I was paranoid.

The thought of meeting my killers had sent a rush of adrenaline to my body I could hardly breathe. I was not a coward but I had to call my friend to cram me down, he was a copper and he was too busy to collect me. As I put my mobile phone down the bus slowly pulled up, the journey was not going to be long, down through the high street down past the Kings Arms which was a pub, along Quarry Way and just around the corner. I did not take the whole journey once the paranoia had worn off I got off half way and decided to walk it was easier breathing in the fresh air rather than trying to breathe on a stuffy old bus. I had started to remanence It was dark I liked the night all the lights it reminded of a journey that I went on when I was a kid. I was walking with my mother she was an old fashioned lady, rich and stuck up I was only five at the time. My father was a solider right up until he died he was always drinking and reasonably aggressive, He was tall like six foot so it seemed. The thoughts were there only for a second and they surpass nicely as I got into a walking pace. I got busy walking the journey home and I was counting the sign posts and my steps.

What I saw was that was the best part of the journey I had decided. That is when I realized that I came from an extremely rich family I do not know all the details, although only that my great great uncle went to Harvard in America that was the very best university at this time and he mixed and befriended the very best.

While I was walking and thinking about these things I saw the most beautiful girl, she had dark hair, slim in stature, she was carrying a hand bag and she was walking a dog. Form what I could see it was a British bull dog.

Her beauty was astounding I could not miss the opportunity the ask this girl out I shouted across the road to her she was definitely the most beautiful girl I had ever seen. However, I had only seen the back of her head, a bag and the back of her leather jacket at the first moment.

When I got home I walked into the hall way stepping over the mail on the floor. I took of my leather jacket and made my way upstairs to my bed room got undressed got into bed and pulled

the duvet cover over me tightly clothes still on.

That evening that is when it started, my whole body began to ache, I had the cold sweats, a fever.

I began to hear voices. I could not feel my feet or my hands I started to weep I thought I was going

blind. The weeping went on for around an hour. My head ached so much I had to go to the fridge to get an ice pack, it did not help I threw the ice pack down I was beginning to get angry. That's when something else happened me and it started a conversation I was in a mess I felt hot all over I opened the windows in the bedroom.

I knew I could only help myself from the very beginning. I did not tell many people this but I was a drunk an alcoholic I waited and waited for the night to come, and I was hoping that it was not going to rain. I noticed that there was total silence around me not a bird in the sky or the sound of a roaring car engine passing by. There was a slight wind. I looked over my shoulder first the right then the left, I had the feeling that I was being watched. You that feeling. I checked the time, even though the experience would only last a few minutes it seemed like hours. I walked up to the circles and took a deep breath this time with my clothes on as I was outside then the voices keep on mentioning it old thoughts they were all acting like they knew something they said so much in so little time. Something happened while I was I the circles while I was meditating one second I was in the future then a split second I was taken deep into the past to relive the past but not realizing at that point the future had disappeared and I could feel it I was trapped. My only thought was to keep on meditating. I found myself reliving everything I experienced in the past, but what was different what was I supposed to change. I thought about it a lot as I was sitting there. As I flowed through my mind I could visualize everything. I was sure that I was here to change something. I went father back. Everything seemed in order everything was the same my bet there was nothing maybe I was just being paranoid I could see that everything from that point was the past and had already happened. As I watched it was like watching a film through the mind of myself of the experiences of the years that I had be through. The cat and the seagull were there also watching me in the past. I reached out trying to touch myself by walking into myself I did not responded but I acknowledged this. Now I was watching

everything and listening too. Every word and sentence I said from the very first vision to my very last verb. Why had I been sent back here and why was

I watching the past. I decided that I

to leave the circle not knowing that I would bring the thoughts and pitchers with me. As I was watching myself I did what was usual and jump on the bed leaning back and crossing my legs. I was moving fast. It was like watching a video film in fast forwards if you could imagine The images finally slowed down.   Just after this they said they were leaving but they took off their shoes and stood by the door it had started raining and I could not imagine them walking out into the pouring rain. There had to be a theory to this unsolved phenomenon. I could only imagine that they were not from this planet.

I closed my eyes and went into myself and asked my soul to follow

and that is when things got complicated I had not yet figure it out but I was going too.
I was told while I travelled in my soul that the person whom

Chapter29 Feeling the cold

The person doing the talking was me in the future pretty grim I think he was or should I say I was a messenger this was going to happen ten years from now. But again I was not sure. Was that really me.
At first I thought it was god the way I spoke, the way I had dressed I was in all white attire. Looking on the religious side of things I could have been an angel, sateen, an angel of death, god, the holy ghost, or even Jesus Christ oh yes and not forgetting aliens.
I came out of my mind I received a message I had to look at the term player what did this mean I know it means whatever it is it knows everything about everything and what the term everything is.
The voices in the back ground became extremely polite there was a voice that which I truly fell in love with. If this was the voice of god I was truly in the right place again but this time it was different this time the princess was not so forth coming. And again the princess was not sop welcoming. It took me

every verb in my body to convince her that I was from the earth. I knew deep down that she really knew. Within a few minutes the princess became polite again.

Once I had established what I was experiencing. Everything even the beat of my heart came to peace. Once I had written this down the voices departed. I went down stairs it was early morning by the time I had finished. I was walking down my stairs in the corridor when there was a knock my door. I opened the door keeping my face partially hidden and my feet were braced against it. It was gate and down the street. I was going to throw the letter on the floor but somehow I managed to hold on to it. It was in a medium sized envelope, white in stature and it felt like it was worth something I hesitated to open it.

I went back upstairs got onto my bed it was large bigger that a two sleeper I liked my space. Especially in bed there are something that enjoy sharing your sleep time with you.

I sat back and closed my eyes it took me a few minutes to settle that's when I was at my most powerful then it happened I began to travel through my eyes into my mind there was somebody there they had not given up their identity there were two of them I could see both of them standing there they were both male the first male said to my surprise did I get the letter then he said I know you have it in front of you the second character just stood there. There was an amazing flush of color steaming through my soul red and greens purple and orange. I asked them a question what do they want, there was a large splutter a cough and them another sputter then finally he started to tell me. He began with opening the letter I could not believe it, a letter from the president so he was one of the figures in my mind that whom I was talking with it stated in the letter that the other figure could not be mentioned due to spiritual reasons but I have reason to believe that it that he was called the 25th one of 25. I opened my eyes as I was getting tired as I already knew what was coming next. I took a deep breath and the journey began again. While I was walking I saw the girl again the same girl and again it was exactly the same as before I knew that she was on the bus before she got off. I ran after her calling out her name this time she stopped and turned around. This time she said hello back when we spoke gore awhile and this time she gave me her number and said call her when I had time.

We spoke for hours discussing all kinds of things where the planets money was going and was it going to the right people other people with the same ability s as ourselves

was it god we were speaking through and how we had to keep our thought s pure so we were safe from sateen and angels. I had to repeat some of the things to myself just to take them in.

I could feel the heat I asked him what that was he said it was fire it was a fire of coldness I had the lack of concentration which was leading me to sweat cold. I looked up there was a coffee drink in front of me it was large in a white kind of triangular shaped mug. That's when the vision had finished I opened my eyes.

That's when I met my other me

I came across as very polite that's when it was revealed to me that I was going to meet a princess.

which one I said gratefully she was going to take you into her eyes. I was told quite a few things about her but before my other self-left I did not give myself the name of this princess. I kind of made it up what the experience should be called it needed a title in the end everything needs a title I came up with real life cross dream experience I could feel her power from here she was in love with me. As I recall the princess was dressed in white but from a distant as she approached my mind her garments changed into a flurry of colors. The feeling was unreal I found it hard to except at first but the thought was so powerful I had no choice but to bow down to it.

I could look into her eyes, she was perfect, she had dark hair perfectly combed. I could not take my mind of her eyes they looked so pure that's when I feel in I was going to ask her for her hand, she already knew this feeling of being there with her was like nothing I could imagine. The vision slowly past I fell into sadness then that's when she spoke to me it was sweet to hear her voice. I come from the planet on the right. That was cool and dangerous.

she spoke with elements she was extremely well spoken.

That was enough for me for now that was the third vision of the day although by the end of the evening I was back in my room I had spent about three days' and this was me forth night that i had

meditated myself across the other side of the planets Ian it was addictive. I gathered my thoughts again, I placed myself down on my bed and closed my eyes. I was moving fast in my mind for a few minutes that's when the journey I was taking stopped. I looked around myself nothing but sand, at the first instants I thought I was in Africa, the sun it was out and it was extremely hot I looked around up and down then into the distant I was on the edge of a desert. that's when I saw a kangaroo I was in Australia. I was hesitant to take a step forwards to see if the ground was hard enough to take me, as I did looking out into the distant I saw a figure it was walking towards me. When he got close enough he stopped and put his hand upon my shoulder. He said nothing at first and I was quick to question him.

I was meeting another president he did not seem to bothered and I asked me why I had summons him to his desert. After a great pause he spoke he said that there was going to be a great war he said that his country had become corrupt and that the people within a few years will turn against each other and that there were many things wrong and he wanted more help from me to correct this how could I help he said I was to take up the power.

There was already wars in the middle east he said that he would meet me in Africa he kept on mentioning the wars of the past and he also said that there was to many corrupt men in power and there will be another time when their own mind will destroy themselves in the background I could hear sirens and the sound of the wind began to get have disturbed me and I had to bring myself back.

I looked out of the the window from my bed the police had parked up outside it seemed very quiet or maybe it was just me. The thought of the Police car outside was preying on my brain as if I was not disturbing enough, this time I got out of my bed I was still tired I closed my eyes the police car had gone and smiled and went back to sleep but it was not long before something went wrong some someone had tried to contact me while I was asleep this was forbidden, it was a rule according to the letter which was the sent. I had the letter under my pillow where it was safe

I had fallen into a deeper sleep in this particular dream, and a dream is different to a vision I do not know much about dreams or visions really but in this was knew I looked up and to my surprise I was surrounded by people on one side of me was a panel there was for people next to each other and they were seated on different levels they were smartly dressed and they were talking amongst themselves. On the left of me was a girl she was small she wore or should I say she was dressed his smartly to except she wore a cloak it was large and looked heavy and on the other side was a tramp holding a sign with his name on it. It said homeless and hungry and had his name on it in big letters, I kept on telling myself that what occurred was everything that had happened before I had somehow managed to write it all down. I sat there in confusion. But there had to be a reason why I was trying to convince myself. I wanted to close my eyes but the thought of mediating why meditating felt too dangerous. My story was now recurring everything that had happened in the future had become my past. I kept on thinking why was I sent back, way back. I could see it was all going to happen again. I could not make out what he was all about then she spoke. He believes that he was the god of war, quoting that he was a poor fellow that welded a bus pass and could not afford his travel but where was this all relevant. It was no, it was just part of the game something to determine that the devil was real and he was still amongst some of us, she went on what if he had a job.

What was I supposed to do, I looked cross at the old man he began to look more and more familiar he was handing under this beard
it was not until I realized that the old tramp was me in some kind of future I took s few steps closer until I was right up to his face. He looked at me I knew those eyes. had found part of myself and I seemed to be on trial I took a closer look at him again and made sure that it was me I was sure. I did not say a word.
It seemed that I had been there before except this place was becoming more and more unfamiliar and the people in it were becoming more and more unsettled. The girl refused to stop questioning the old man which supposedly was supposed to be me into leaving eventually the girl gave in the old man became powerful a sparkle of light came from his body and he disappeared. He had died. I fell to the floor it was painful watching yourself die. That was it I had seen enough. Had enough have you she replied I. I was still on the floor when she said it, she was convinced that she had destroyed us both that when I awoke. I was sweating what that was I knew that one day I am going to meet my maker if it be an old man or a little girl I had a rival this was quite common apparently in the realms of meditation. What I saw was a dream so nothing really happened but there was a possible chance that when I get old ill properly become a victim of hell like every person.

It was time to find myself as teacher, but first I had to bring myself back that's when I opened my eyes I came back slowly.

I jumped up and looked in the mirror my face had changed I had aged about ten years that's when I realized what was happening why did I not notice it before I went to my bedroom and opened the letter that the president had sent me while you meditate instead of growing younger you will grow older each time you use your mind in this way this letter is a warning and an invitation to join us do not be discouraged this letter also has the rules you will grow young again but only in time.

It was time for me to make more time for myself the whole situation of growing old before you grow young was beginning to get to me I did not take me long to figure out that I had been leaving myself for dead while meditating in fact the thought was so strong I became light headed for a whole hour or two and worried with the thought. This continuous light headedness had happened before I remember the girl I meet while walking home I felt so bad because she did not answer me I just felt like dying this was the fifteenth time I had felt drowsy now after the meditation, I was counting and I wanted to rested my head on the toilet bowl a few minutes later I was sick the smell of puke filled the bowl and the taste was in my mouth I wanted to get up but I could not the only thing I could do was put my fingers down my throat an puke up again just to get rid of the feeling.

After this experience I knew that travelling through my mind could be seriously dangerous as for me things we're looking a little bit dark maybe it's a start of a new journey which is supposed to be light. I walked out of my house the wind was blowing in my hair I pulled my scarf around my face I had not been in the fresh air for outside for around a month consistent meditation I could feel my soul sucking the darkness into my mind. I thought to myself I have been to pretty fantastic places. I had not eaten for a month or drank anything I did not realize how thirsty I had become. I was in such a good mood I decided to walk the shopping Centre. I had eaten everything in the house the cupboards were empty. I liked to keep a low profile the first thing that I went for when I got there was some booze that was not so pure so. I'll try anything once just like everybody else I looked around the shop floor I found all the food that I wanted.

I had got some shopping good s and payed at the till the lady was quite nice nobody said a thing but it was like everybody knew. I walked home, sun slowly disappeared behind some clouds I was left with just the cold air.

The next thing that was going to happen to me was that I was going to meet her boyfriend I went into deep meditation as soon as I got home, I was trailing the journey I knew it's every turn how long the roads were. When the next turn was going to be. Past the Japanese restaurant. That's when I saw her the chick with the leather jacket and hand bag the guy whom was sitting next to me must have been a dreamer he did not even notice her. Hold on driver I said I want to get off. I jumped off at the next turning. What a gift I bumped straight in to her she dropped her bag I apologized and helped her pick her things up. I'm really sorry I said. She did not speak English but she bowed a couple of times to say thank you. She was shy I called out what's your name but I seemed to scare her off. I opened my eyes and brought myself back again. I stepped outside for some fresh air.

It was late when I got in I could not believe I was walking around half dead and beat I was not used to it. I was outside for a few hours. The wind got heavy I could feel hitting my face and blowing my scarf around. I bowed my head to stop the wind from blowing my hat off. when I walked it was like I was really fighting the elements. When I got in my home I was greeted.

with load cheers and welcomes, welcome home the voices said I went straight to the toilet. I can't explain the feeling but it was like the room was sucking the light out of the side s of my face the first thing to do is throw up the feeling was that bad and dizzy I was not sick as such I was just over excited I think but this was not good not again. I asked myself when there was quiet I guess the voices were just excited to see me as I was them, they often said they missed me they were friendly but there was a feeling for this. I was just going to sit down when the worst pain I could imagine hit me. I knew that I was going to feel something I had the same weird feeling that something was going to happen all day long. I picked up the phone struggling to see the numbers on the dial. I had blurred vision it was not good.

I rang the local doctors there is as no answer I threw myself on to my knees and closed my eyes and prayed to god. I had tooth ache it was bloody painful and cold sweats, by the time I found a doctor I could not be seen. They were deadly serious about their business I had not realized but I had missed two appointments so they stuck me off apparently. I'll find another good doctor I told myself. The pain was not receding and I was desperate and in pain, I got lucky. I found one on the edge of town. I left my home to go outside. The bright lights hit my eyes that's when I realized that I needed something they were simply a brand small, and came in many brands I wanted a pair of sun glasses I wanted to know if they could exist in me knew world I do not know what to call it so I just call it the system. What I did not tell you that before I meditate I have to stripe naked it is the way.

I found a pair most expensive plastic sun glasses they were dark and made me feel like a real star I walked straight in to the waiting room to the left of me was a toothbrush cabinet with toothbrushes in it and tooth paste, the room was full of people I tried to look intelligent as I sat down waiting.

and all the posters were scattered across the wall it was like a teenager's bedroom, it had been at least ten years since I had had a tooth ache I did not like the feeling but does anyone.

I could not wait any longer the pain was now unbearable I closed my eyes what's the answer I said it was like I was on a train the

flashbacks mixed with dreams of paracetamol to ease the pain.

I kind of thought that the dentist was going to take me in to an otherworld. I was slow realizing that I could mess with anybody. It was kind of paranoia. I was quite surprised with the turn out in the dentist. I had been waiting for about fifth teen minutes that is when I had the idea of jumping the que. There was an old man sitting right next to me I needed to know his name so I made polite conversation with him and at the end of the conversation I asked him his name shook his hand as this happened his name was called out I stood up slowly waving the old man back down on to his seat but this time it was different instead of the old man sitting back down he stood still waving his walking stick at everybody especially me and called out that it was his turn. And claimed to the sector that I was jumping the que I left in a hurry. as I took his place to go in to the surgery room. As we started the removal of my tooth I began to realize that We did not get along in fact we hated each other even if I was polite she made sure that she hated me in the chair she made it clear. She did not know me it was just her way I always thought of myself now as a star, it was not something I did but it was said that I had changed the shape of the inside of my mind by meditation but I think it was stupid, irresponsible and a childish thing to do. So The power of meditation was beginning to change the shape of my mind. I had to believe it I had seen everything that there was to see in the mind without actually

going anywhere. Of course this was quite serious matter It was better than a science lesson I had seen everything that there was to see and I had been everything that I was going to be. I looked
chapter30 Somebody again

out of my window it gave myself a piece of my mind. I could see that the papers had heard, it looks like the media had got my stories. I Went to the front door not to invite them in but to pick up the morning paper. As I did I found a picture of myself on the front cover it read Actor goes psycho with meditation trouble. I had not sold them the story however I tried to explain that they were only dreams. The cameras were at my door now as I stood there saying nothing they were at my home now day and night. I could not move, eat, or even sleep. I was pretty cool with this as I had experienced this thing before it was cool and dangerous.

I walked into the front room everybody was there the old man from the trail who was a tramp. the girl, the girl that grilling the old tramp who I think was me was now having a word with the president and the 25th. It was a great debate. I closed my eyes for a second then in that instance I knew that I was in the wrong place at the wrong time. It was Just seconds before I was going to start making my way out of the place I blacked out through tiredness.

When I awoke I found myself tucked up in bed although. I was acting if nothing had happened as I was trying to find the truth. I asked myself a question why was I here I asked. Don't worry they said you will be all right. I did not know where I was or whom I was speaking with. The only thought was of the girl there was an image that I could not get out of my head.
whoever she was she was caring for me I know, I looked around, in front of me was a mirror I struggled to sit up to it, when I did I smiled I could see clearly I was in the right hands, there was lip stick marks on my face and about my lips. I wondered who she was then she walked in it was her the princess. The princess explained what I could not believe, it was if they had brain washed my mind.
After this I could not think about anything else apart from the princess which whom I was in love with and still do and always will.

When I had meditated myself back to myself and got home. David the tramp was in my kitchen turning out my cupboard looking for something to eat.
take it easy said I reached out to touch him on the shoulder, that's when he spoke in one word he told me everything. I needed to know about everything in one thought the vision that he sent me raced through my mind at millions of miles per hour it was like riding a slip steam building over and over building the pictures in my mind until it was full.

I fell to the floor I was exhausted, when I got up he was gone and so was the food. I was about to crack up for some reason I kept on having accidents I took my jacket off it was ripped and looked dirty and went upstairs what' s the reason that I am being treated so badly. I had to ask myself if I had done anything wrong, then it came to me that the voices they have not been in touch which was problem a good enough reason to think that they were the reasons that I was in so much pain taken in to consideration that I never said to them that they had to leave so where were they.

One thing that I know if the media got hold of my stories what would they think. What would they write, well the night was young I had not felt like this for a long time but then I had a few bad nights it was not that bad. The fact that my dreams were scaring me is that why I woke up crying it was like I was a little baby waiting for my mummy to come and wake me and pick me up but that was not going to happen. Then there was good therapy but that was wearing off. I had to find to something to impress myself this experience was coming to the end and the whole system was on the brink of destruction. After years of meditation and preys and enlightening visions at least I knew that there was no other person but God that I would like to talk too.

The little people had become my new subject and my main concern I would sit there for weeks on end day after day just waiting to hear from them.
That night I lay there upon my bed
in the same room I was a little reluctant to close my eyes I was frightened of what I thought of what I was going to see.
It's funny because if I told you that my best friend was in the same room as me watching me. watching over me.

I would be telling him to turn down the music or turn on the radio it was enough to drive you nuts. I closed my eyes and took of my clothes and put the sun glasses on and sat crossed legged on the floor I closed my eyes and it had begun I found myself in the same room as my cat the one that died I was sitting there on the floor I could feel this kind of silky feeling then it just walked out, it was my cat. I don't believe it who told you. I asked it not expecting an answer it replied everybody knows. even the ground that you sit upon. At this point I Knew the cat was in on it, he could speak human.

True it said even though they hate you I'll be honest it does not mean a thing. The same thing had happened again as I remember going into the garden at this point nothing changed.
In fact, they do not care. Which in my eyes is disobedient?
The cat walked in as slowly as a panda his speech was somewhat different now he was a clever cat he was shut the door after him I had no choice but to shout out to it my words were that I could meditate myself through that.

Three months past I had meet the cat on numerous occasions he spoke of great riches and worldly things to be won in the spiritual world he often boasted that he had nine lives' always said it was a gift to be a human for me or anybody in a matter of fact.

A few more week past but the cat's visit's had become less and less than the cat stopped appearing. I wondered where he had gone. I was so silly I did not think. It was not until I got another white envelope letter from the president that I found out that the

the cat had slowly past away again and was going to be replaced.

Replaced I said to myself replaced with whom. I did not take the subject up again it was too personal I remembered the cat it would sit on my bed without saying a word. The cat was a smart creative creature he will be dearly missed.

when I began to write I was busy writing my third novel it was big bigger than the first two I wrote that I had done as I had thought about his thoughts. As this is my cat and I was going to meet him on the spiritual plane I felt excited. He returned but something awful had happened he returned but he returned as a killer he killed somebody and was sent straight to hell.

I saw him briefly before this terrible incident had happened I did not ask any personal questions as I remember he just walked in without saying a word and laid on my bed. He did not speak which was unusual He seemed different subdued the look on his face was not normal. His whiskers were wet and he could not stop licking his paws. I took a closer look at him his fur it looked rugged and hard not soft and shiny. the dirty deed was done he did not know anything more about it I asked him to meditated with me as he did before but he refused. There was a look of glee in his eyes that's when I forced myself to throw him off the bed and put him outside. He wondered in again and again this happened at least three times away.

It was going to be one of those days I just knew I was told by a phone message that I was going to be baby sitting at exactly five O clock. I looked at the clock that's great I said to myself I had time to quickly get dressed as you do, jeans, t shirt, smart shoes what's the time five thirty or there about go just got time to catch the sun set I could watch that sky line all day. I might see a flying saucer or a space ship, all try and see if I can spot the number on a plane will be the little alien on the wing I'm just going to get my binoculars said to myself the weathers good and the sky looks good too I was trying to be protective It was not as if was trying to protect the neighbors with this impassive attitude watching the sky's lights dim the winter nights and early

Chapter31 Dressed in black

Afternoons.

I was wrapped up fairly warm but still felt the cold a part from my jeans which were torn in the knees and I had a t shirt and a jumper which I had forgot to mention. My hands were bleeding of the cold weather its always my two hands that's a fact. a star appeared I got all excited.

To me it was way up there I could point to it and just about make it out that's unreal. most of stars were good this one was not an evil star like the cat but it was right above my head it was a glowing, friendly, mature, a baby, I tried my very hardest not to notice but I could not help myself I had to say hello.

And that was it was said that if you disturb one star you disturb them all and that's a lot of stars to be disturbing you but I found that they were happy to be friend me they were happy that I was in control of them. After finding out this knowledge I was tempted to go public my attitude was like a spoilt brat and I knew this and I was always trying to change the way I was thinking.

I might get a response in the end. I went back inside I had just baby sat the stars and I had really enjoyed it.

There was an instant after the experience that I had three further premonitions and two days later I had a virus I passed out again and ended up in the princesses arms she was always happy to see me and I was happy waking up to her. The princess handed me a mirror and asked me to look into it.

I looked in the mirror and pulled an ugly face I did it a bit more until I began to upset myself and smiled the princess. The princess then asked me what I could see. I waited for a moment I said to her that I did not need the mirror to see, she said in a very soft voice just look so I did. I saw myself throwing myself straight on to my knees and asking god for forgiveness. I tried figured out that why was I throwing myself down on my knees and would I actually possibly do it. The princess asked me to practice it. so I practiced it for a minute or two I was a man of my word and of the lord I said she replied wise worlds.

Anyway this great experience I had become one with myself although now my body was aged.
considerable. I was wondering how I was going to turn my myself into the young man again. I went into the kitchen and put some water into a kettle and turned it on. I was making a cup of tea. I had made it as I slowly sipped from the cup I was thinking
What annoyed me the most was it the cat or was it that I was living in town but it was just as noisy in the town as it was in the country side too I do not only know this through my experiences and they thought the same.
I picked up the cup of tea I took one sip of it and poured the rest of it down back into the pot. I then realized that was a waste and I said it to myself. It had begun to rain I could hear the drop lets outside splashing on the the window pane and on the roof that's when the weirdest thing happened to me the clouds departed quickly like there was another storm was brewing it was like a storm on top of a storm the clouds were moving quickly. I look up a sat down in a puddle the water was ice cold, I planted my arms and hands down into the grass I was on the grass. I closed my eyes what did it say I can not remember exactly it was a whisper it was something like alpha alphenia the sky's had spoken to me for the first time I had find out what this meant.
It was the week end and the football was on I had put my life aside just to listen to the game I like the football they always seemed up set the commentators I thought me be it was me, the teams were quite excellent and exciting this I what I thought the player I liked most was circus.
The rebuilding of my mind and body was important to me I was not getting any younger yet that was the way most people end up. The music was another thing. I heard this voice it was loud it was spiritual I'm not sick I said I'm not a schizophrenic there was a second person to but you hear things from time to time. Like you
understand. I knew who it was the voices they had finally came back, I turned up the TV
back to watching the football I could not comprehend what I was about to go through
come on boy you know the routine drop them pants they were joking there was about twenty minutes to go but the voices were still persistent they had

prepared themselves I could tell. I was sitting there semi naked on the floor anyway I turned on the TV and sat down cross legged my arms aside of me my hands face looking down on the floor. My eyes became heavy in a desperate When I met Eugene for the second time she had changed not just her temperament but her face she looked different. I noticed straight away that the smile that she used to greet me with had gone and her nippiness and bounciness seemed to be missing. Her hair was also different and her color had changed from brunet to blond. It looked kind of boyish I kind of hid my laughter as I did not want to upset her. I wanted to teller but I could not bring myself to as she already looked upset and my comments would only upset her more. I attempted to turn off the TV but it was too late the voices began their synchronized attack the sensation left me sitting up right it sent my body into body in to an over whelming fit of love the whole vision leaped me on to the TV. could see everything but it did not stop there the voices had entered the program too. And they were being spoken about this it made me angry the colors in my mind began to change from black to yellow then too green and orange I was travelling faster than the speed of light. Where I was going I could not tell you at this moment I was surfing in the air for about half an hour.

All I could here was music the voices had entered the radio all I heard was can you hear the music can you hear that. when I landed I briskly ran my hands over my body there was a lady she was on the TV. It was a film that I was watching, there was a new feeling in my body, it was the first time I had mediated with the TV on it was dangerous even more so the radio was on in the
background. I was in ecstasy, all I know is that I was fond of her, it was not that teenage crush. And I was not the shy type but I was still a virgin and quite inexperienced. It was not just the film stars now it was the radio stars as well that's when the doorbell rang I struggled to my feet bringing myself back and hurried to the main door clumsily knocking over a vase on to the floor from off its table.
Express delivery a voice called out from behind the door. The mail it was a white envelope. What is the time I asked myself I looked down at my watch 3pm exactly it was the president I bet? I staggered on my feet and walked back to my room the I was right. What was the warning.

this time I took the envelope and opened it up in large bright letters I said turn off the TV and turn the music off. I had no choice but to take his advice. I was a sucker for perfection in a specific way. I had been taught through my soul. It was sex, sex, drugs, and more sex. oh yes and who was getting richer and richer I was every day I have thought about it you no playing this relationship was the most genius thing, what a wonderful thing to my soul. The voices had stop all I could do is sit there exhausted again.

The doorbell rang I could not be bothered to answer it so I shouted out I am not in. The doorbell rang again go away I said calmly it rang once more I forced myself to my knees the sweat poured of my body Jesus it was my mum hi I greeted her doing that meditation again. I said nothing
all I could focus on was my mum I had to get her outside the house. She said I looked a state I agreed. I grabbed a towel from the bathroom. And walked her to the kitchen. It was not a long visit and a few hours later she left. I chose to sleep the rest of the day.

The next morning "hello darling she said haply what are you doing here I let myself in I thought there was nobody in."
"I see just having a snoop ".
"oh no do you think".
"I just came around to make sure you are all nice and tidy" she said that in a shimmering but sensitive kind of thought
Then there was another voice "hello"

"who's there" called.
It's you knew house mate do you know the date.
You must be Eugene that s right she said with a smile and sticking out her hand I shook it she did not notice the sweat she never caught on.
But I knew somehow that she knew what I had been doing then she noticed your sweating she said
but before I had a chance to explain mother butted in
he is a mediator.
Sweat she replied "that's good"
that's when it happened I began to sweat cold oh no I said again.
Five minutes into the conversation she noticed

are you all right your sweating err she said trying not to notice it she them wiped her hand down her
blouse.
You are sweating profusely are you all right
I am yes I sweat a lot sometimes.
You should go lay down. Do you have a tempter?
I do yes.

"The football dam it what the score". I had forgotten the football was on which gave me an excuse to quickly change the subject from how sweaty I was to the football results.
   "2-0 I think."
   "who scored".
   "it was that foreign player".
   they begin to laugh.
   "what s up".
   "it's your face you look well funny".
   "just tell me the score".
   "look we have done it"
they laugh again." that's it gets out that's enough ".
"your throwing me out wait a minute this is my house you have only just got here".
The music was blearing out but I was not really listening to it. All I could here was my house mate taking about me above the music to herself. I wanted to think that they were that's when the oddest thing I thought that his mother went home
I went to the window and made sure it was shut. At least I knew who I was a fashion star, role model and movie star.

Going back to the football arsenal came back from being 2 goals down. I did not disturb my new house mate again looked out of the window it was night time I have to admit she had quite a presents I kind of felt safe around her I looked at her resume model and role model it looked pretty
good. The next morning, I went to the window I looked out of the window their she was undressing in the garden first her top then her t -shirt. I turned away I had to be crazy not to peak.
I thought for a moment that I was a really lucky guy. It was me again I'm

sure I was being drawn in some kind of super power I do not mean to turn the radio or the TV. It was a luxury for me to have music on. I wanted to know what kind of adventure she had in mind. She dived into the pool
The day went past quickly there I looked out the window the love was still there she was sitting so the in the garden. Eugene was sitting singing. That is when I stumbled across the idea to put a film
on. the film I chose was a romance film do you think she would catch on was. I wanted to pull her. The movie that I put
was an epic adventure and romance movie I pushed the pause button.

Eugene was still sat there in the garden she was still singing it sounded good then the style changed rapidly to a rap song I will not go any further that. I sat back on the sofa put my arms on my head you could clearly see what was going to happen I was going to fall in love with her.
She came in and sat down next to me she never said a word but I was desperate to break the silence.
The conversation I wanted to start left my mind. I got up a went outside to practice what I was going to say to her quickly. she shouted out a few seconds later to see if I was OK. I then reversed the question are you, I shouted back.

Okay I silently said to myself the window cleaner had turn up. I wanted to know wanted to know the ins and outs of this chick you know what makes her click. Then I realized that it could be easier than I first thought I could meditate myself in to her universe. About fifteen minutes later she had walked in and sat down in front of the film. I had gone to my room. I am going

ask the man at the top I said quietly to myself. She sat there watching the film I could hear her playing it from my room.
Things were getting more tense then the sweats began I had my answer from the top of my head.
I sat down I was semi naked I put the sun glasses on, she was not an easy person to find.

s

Eventually she gave in I got into her mind I could see her clearly she was golden she liked money

she considered herself a movie star, a film prodigy and an actor and play write. She said when I asked her what she liked to be called she said mogul. She was also well trained she was a sixth Dan karate and artist. She was everything.

 except she did not have the big mansion the fast cars what she did have was a good home and lots friends which I understood.

I slowly went in looking for her friends I had found them, the first was this guy called Richard they met at a bar in Soho. He was fit and young I meant that in a good way. He was tall in stature there

was a dark side to him he said that his brother had committed suicide

I could feel her power she as strong it was scary but she was so pure in her heart. Trying to find a way out of her was going to take me to

the edge.

by the time I had finish it was 4. of pm she was on the phone

I know mum but he understands me the conversation went on me why, what. His stature no he does not look like a gorilla, no he has not got a belly either yes of course he's had a drop before.

About 6 ft. and holy the conversation ended with that.

What was going to happen to me I said I properly go to hell for all my sins.

I just hoped that she would make to the same heaven as me. We met in the hallway we practically bumped into each other that s when we hit it off. We stood there talking for hours. We were coming

to the end of the conversation the last questions she said after great debates we discussed how many heavens there where she said none I said seven I did not want to discuss the subject any more so I said I want to take a break, my jaw was aching from all the taking. But she went on for hours more, I was impressed but unsure that I should answer her questions the answer to these questions would only upset me. In the end she said she loved me and Jesus Christ. Well that took all day I said to myself and briskly walked to my bedroom

The next day early in morning I woke up I was still feeling tied I tried to get back to sleep I tossed turned and fell out of my bed. That's when I asked myself another unorthodox question what was sleep
and where did it come from. Why do we need more as we get older and where does the conscious come from and how the soul knows and control I know what I was doing was travelling through my conscious going to place to place?

I had many visions and dreams, they take me way back to the days when had travelled across to the America I must had been there sometime in my last life. somehow we are spiritually connected.
The dreams I had were getting worse and harder and harder to understand I was thinking a lot of people would disagree that the dreams and visions I am having are true I am not knowing the
exact truth about what I see and hear.

All I can say whatever it is it is well hidden inside of you. It was when I had awoken I had soon realized what had done. My first thought was to wash and clean myself up. The second thought was I wished I had a dream well I hoped for God s sake it was a dream but it was not it was very real. I was dreaming about a dream as an I sat in the chair the thoughts were streaming into the point that I had blocked my own mind stopping the thoughts and images I wanted to learn how to act. I wanted to be an actor, the thought was overwhelming. It was taking me to new kinds of places. My thoughts wondered around and around all day long that's when Eugene walked in
I could smell booze I smiled your drunk but then the tears came to my eyes.
I felt my flesh crawl for the second time the first was this morning that's when it all came flooding back my memory was on fire, picture after picture I sat there watch her well into afternoon

so what is your style
there's no style to it just be yourself are your gay it helps if you are a little bit Kamp
I can do Kamp

relax breathe as I did this I Totally loosed the plot I could hear here as clear as day acting but I Had fallen again as for what I could or see was very very different I was receiving messages at a big level I had received letter after letter another and another. They were rolling in message after message telling me of the future, where I should go, with whom and who I would be helping. I had just been told who the 25 were as I did not really notice them as I did not understand them they had never approached me in my mind until now. They always seemed to be around me when the president was there. I guess you could call them body guards or advisors. I did not notice them at first but as they moved they seemed to me to be hovering what were they were ghosts of some kind. When they spoke they all huddled together as I recall they all spoke at the same time and moved at the same time. I did not want to ask due to my shyness and amazement.

It was the first time that I was going to use my mind to defend most of the spiritual world, could you imagine a war of minds it to me was cool as I did not take it seriously at first and a short time after I had received message that I realized that it was true and that it was serious. I sent a message to my wife and child telling them of the messages that were sent. They replied that they already knew and it was on their behalf, I replied again that there were many questions to be asked and answered especially. As my mind kicked in and still being in the room with Eugene again this time it was different. I was now looking for the president to confirm what my wife the princess had written I could not find him anywhere. In fact, it was the total opposite as I was told that the war had finished over forty years ago and the planets were at peace. I could tell that this was going to be a hard one to explain. I needed to know who I was speaking with. I then brought myself back. It was like nothing had happened I was still in the room talking about acting. I continued Eugene never noticed as it was only a few minutes which seemed like hours or even days.

the lesson went on for hours we were having such a good laugh I was like it was meant to be there was a connection between us we were defiantly meant for each other. We both ended up on the floor I had her in my arms.

Later on the two other house mates were about to arrive I left the door open so they could just walk
in there was a loud hello I replied with a shout come through.
Nice to see you
your welcome

so what have you been doing

not a lot she said

come on I'll show you around I showed them the whole mansion then I took both of the them down

stairs to the games room. The games room was my personal space I made it quite clear that it was a no go area and to get in you needed an invite from me. It was only for computer players. I had the latest games consoles and about 1010 games nobody had a collection like me. I could use a computer fully by the time I was 11 yr. s old. I had hacked into several banks and made them offer me money, by the time I was 16 I was imprisoned in a youth policy treatment Centre I also had a brutally knackered nervous system the computer ate me and my nerves and that was my greatest achievement. I continued.

nobody, I was half way through a conversation that would be a great achievement I was saying but I reckon that not only would he open the front door but he would answer the back door as well and on top of this he would do the cooking and the cleaning to. I was just complimenting my two new house mates they were so polite and tidy I had to remember my manners.

I had actually had enough for one day Dave was OK so was the guru and so was Eugene. I wanted to know the ins and outs of the guru he had a spiritual name but how spiritual was he I said.

That was to come later first I had to get rid of my old memory. So I told the lord to unload my old

memory it was an amazing feeling my soul came out above me and touched my mind the whole front

of my forehead flicks it's self-up into the air I had lost my mind again there I had been unloaded now I asked the lord to save me just one more thing left to do is to close my eye s just for a minute to see what was in there.

A cigarette and a nice glass of wine to celebrate I went down into my wine cellar and picked up a bottle of champagne. When I got back from the wine cellar I grabbed a couple of glasses from the kitchen and walked to the living room.

What s on TV I asked pulling up a chair and popping the bottle open it made Eugene jump? The football was on. Who's playing.

Arsenal

what again.

The monsters were coming home I do not know why I said that maybe it was a child hood thing. Eugene wanted to talk about her child hood. The guru was there listening and advising her he was a good listener. The Guru just sat there we were all intrigued. I even began to feel a little sorry it was a sad tale for someone who had such a great influence in people I could see her destroying herself I had to stop her we were no longer strangers the doors of our pasts were going to be opened and our mind's interacted and closed.
The Guru was making us all smile so I sent him down to the wine cellar to fetch me another couple of bottles. I had decided that we were getting drunk. It was easier to ease the pain when you were drunk and you can never remember what was said the next morning.

We sat and talked for hour each of us taking a turn I was good

Chapter32 A few musicians

I felt like somebody again I got so drunk just wanted to talk about everything except on this occasion I left the meditation out of it
I really thought hard weather or not I should share the secrets.

I had to make the excuse of wanting to get another bottle from cellar to escape telling them the truth
that is when I got a message from the delivery boy. There was a knock at the door I staggered to the front door and opened it there was man standing there holding out his hand in it was a letter he thanks me and left. I opened it quickly and nervously said to myself "damn presidents going to war". It read after great consideration I have put many thoughts and after the long process of many talks and discussions we have come to the theory that we have no choice but to declare war on the world you are with me we want total destruction of the human race It was sighed I turned the letter over.

Well the spiritual world was going to war where will the players go if there's going to be a war.

It was a joke I'm sure the spirit was not as strong as the human body it can only sit and torment.

I think he is fighting a losing battle or he is going win one.

I waited for everybody to go to bed I stripped off and got on my bed I sat in my normal position and closed my eyes and waited and waited then suddenly with a second I was there it was it was true there was going to be war. I looked around there were body's everywhere children crying I took a child right up into my arms her tears escaladed down her face I asked what her name was she said Noah

what happened here I asked her she explained.

 I sat down by a rock closed my eyes I was going to find the president and 25th and see if we could find a suitable answer for the problem. I had sat there for about three days the guys in the house were getting concerned because I had been out of my room. It took me a few more days I was looking for a place to hide but everything was destroyed. The best that I could was to do was to hide in an ordinary old hut I was dragging the body's in body after body I moved from province to province. I was going into shock the body's and the destruction and everything it was too much to take. They had ruined everything and if this was going to be in my mind I was going to be worried for a long time. In a way it was a lesson and I made a note that I would tell my children and they would tell there's and so on.

When my house mate knocked on my door I just had to tell them that I was busy and that they should go away

Eugene became force full I had to convince her that I was alright and spoke to her through my bedroom door. I was using the time to find them the war torn victims.

Meanwhile Eugene was going on about something completely different I had bump right into her mind, all I could see was the thought and it was a man, he said loved her well in fact it was totally the opposite I could see that now I was in love with her. I had never raised my voice but I was slowly temped. Who was this man where did he come from and why was he after my wife? I have become everything you said that I would become and it is your fault. In fact, all I did was act and I think you made me feel real jealous but in fact

I was not ready to perceive. I locked her inside of me she was extremely hard and I wished upon the hardness of her character which I had created in side of me would not die. Having been slightly side tracked only in hearing what had been said. I fear that I may have over visited her.

I was done for the day I got up got dressed and walked out of my mansion and went into town to the café when I got there was no nowhere to sit I had order end my coffee and I was trying to put the morning' s thoughts behind me. I was standing up it was like being head boy. all over again everybody was welcoming me with open arms. I got a big hug from some bloke then there were cheers and singing people just going crazy. I have not been patted on
the back so many times before. The cafe finally empty's about dinner time and I found a seat I looked on the menu and took a sip of the coffee. Just before I sat down I thought I was going to cry was everybody in the cafe actually was laughing I said to myself I must have missed the joke where they laughing at me. I asked myself. I could not express the feeling of my luck everything had slowed right down in my mind. It was like when   you watch old people walk it was like it was in slow motion and the crazed man being falsely fed by a lunatic even worst it was like taken your medication, do it quickly I had to admit that the medication tastes like it had gone off even which a slow glass of water.

I coughed and swallowed deeply and then coughed some more I rubbed my chest. That is when knew
the pain was so abrupt it was like taking a bullet or worse, although the pain was not in my mouth like a broken tooth but was like a swift pain straight to my heart I thought I would say that I have falsely fallen away from the girl that I had loved. I passed out.

The next evening, I had woken up sitting up right. The blanket that I was leaning on was not mine and the man that was sitting on it was not a friend I did not know the man who shared it with me. I looked around all I could see was the old man and a clear white ceiling as I was looking upwards. I asked him if the fruit that was in front of me was mine and if it was not if he would kindly remove it. The voice of the man seemed familiar.

I know you I said speak I want to hear your voice he spoke out after 5 or 6 minutes. I caught on it was the president I could not believe it I was saved. I actually started to laugh it had been the first time in ages. I laughed and laughed it was lucky if anything. That is when they walked in the man that was sitting there the president disappeared to my amazement.

It was going to take me all day to get my head around that I was left with a disgruntled look upon my face. With a new story in my mind I wanted to know where the man went.

It was Dave the guru and Eugene I could not recall her name I started by calling her Debbie
Eugene smiled is that an old girlfriend she said it's me. She smiled again and said come over here lover boy and give me a kiss. I was just about alive when her name came to me
 lips. As she kissed me the life streamed into my body. Time was ticking away I could not make eye contact due to the embarrassment of finding myself where I was. You passed out
I just looked at the clock on the wall. I knew I was in bed and that s about it, I did not know how I got here it took me a while to recognize who the people in front of me were. I asked them if they were my friends all the other people in the room were visitors. I closed my eye s and fell asleep. The next day in the morning I was greeted by Dave he handed me a cup of tea I spilt it over myself straight away I was that weak I could not hold the cup.
That's when the girl walked in I had forgotten how to speak she was not good looking and I was not going to desert my friends. She strolled over she was holding a paper in one hand I could hear her thoughts. That was not the thoughts of a meditator but the thoughts of a street drug user someone who takes mind altering drugs to change the shape of the mind so they could be like me I could see that she was in some kind of pain I know it' s a sad rule but we are taught to dispose of people like that for abusing their spirit. I tried to talk and it was so frustrating I attempted to shout in the process ripping my voice box apart the loudest I could speak now was more or less like a squeak.

I hummed for a while hoping that a word would pop out then this lady walked past Dave was sitting there just talking I was not realize that he was right next to me listening. I had more interest in the people coming and going.

She stopped right in front of me she was not very tall she was fat and slowly spoken she said to me as she passed by my bed I had great respect for the poor they will die first.

Chapter33 Thinking about you

Two second s later a girl walks in dressed in black. Dave the guru said I was to listen to him yeah I

 said go on I'm there I said coolly. I was still struggling to talk at this moment then some old woman started crying and shouting. Her father had just died, she picked up his jacket and removed his wallet and out it in her purse, Dave the guru saw it to he looked at me and asked me if had meant anything to me I had not brought my wallet with me we smiled. Dave the guru was a quiet person he went over to comfort her and basically told her to shut he hell up he was not too remorseful she had got the money. I looked up the word' slowly came to my mouth I could speak again the sentence which came to my mouth the words where you would not understand. I began to smile and I laughed I knew he would understand. The young girl that was hanging around the doormen try helped the old lady and started to comfort her again she was in tears but you could clearly see that she was a money grabber. Then I heard a voice it calmly said.

I vet got tortoise blood, I looked down I believe that there was a little boy boasting to me. He was dressed in a fancy dress costume he said his name was the turtle he was well spoken and told me and Dave the guru that he could not express the way he was feeling although I could hear him swear and curse under his breath as he spoke I was always right it never came to my mind at the time just to shout.

Many people claimed that they knew me and wanted to experience the same as me when I walked outside they said I was walking with the sheep. Suddenly a load of people walked in. A lady in a pink top walk in she dropped her business card on to the table she was given them out to everybody. The lady lent on the dinner tray on one arm. I had never seen her before, she was slim but her head did not go with her body maybe it was her hair cut it was bundled up into a nest and her eyebrows were bushy and her clothes tight with a large chest. And to top it off her glasses were at the end of her nose. What the guru asked. Life insurance she replied. Dave the guru and myself just burst out laughing and sent her away. She was not impressed. It was late I wanted to go home in fact I was going to ask Dave whom had fallen asleep to get me some food there was nothing a good feed. It was a dream the last time I ate out was in the late 90s let the good time roll. Although it was hospital food but beggars cannot be choosers.

There was one time I was at a football do my best friends mum and husband all got drunk and even funnier my best friend sat down to eat and missed his seat. I've got some photographs somewhere. I finally got off my ass

 things in the real world were getting too serious. I was told one day by a voice on a tape message that I was not to do any driving under any circumstances I had not driven since then for a couple of years and the rent that I brought in from the two lodgers gave me enough money to buy a car that is it, the freedom of the road. It was not long before I was on the road I enjoyed driving at night especially though did not go out often I was really ready for a drive. I put the keys into the ignition I was ready to go. I leant back in the racing bucket seat foot on the pedal. Then I stopped being laid back already I put my hands on my head. And that was it driving experience over and done with for the night. In fact, I had not gone anywhere I was too paranoid.

"Go far did you".

"about as far as the drive way".

"why did you buy a car your obviously not going to drive it."

"yes I will just give me time".

"you have had it for weeks."

"you're better off riding an ox".

"maybe in India."

I was dreaming I could hear the police sirens in the background I did not know whether they were real or whether they were part of the dream.

I just wanted to finish the game the boss man told me that the keys had been locked in the car

for the first time I did not understand the dream there was no significant.

I sat in the smokers hut the smell was quite distasteful the taste of my first cigarette for the day. The air was quite humid, I could hear the birds and the traffic surrounding me, the building on the left was a drop in Centre, the door that just slammed was the door to the entrance the smokers room. There patience's all came out one by one they all said hello I stood there silent I did not want to speak and I sure as hell was not going to start making friend's or start talking about my mental problems. I finished my smoke and walked across the hallway. I was about to meet some really crazy people again it had only been a second since I had met the first lot. I fact today I will always say I made some of my best friends on that day. They were good people and clean

and polite they were just mixed up kind of like myself.

They gave me anything I wanted clothe s food, cigarettes and conversation.

There was a man there he was dressed in a black suit jacket he had short hair, scruffy jeans and shoes. His name well I was not sure now as we only met briefly. There was another man he came out side as I was walking in to the building he was dressed the similar jeans t-shirt and trainers.

I wanted to know if clothes made a difference in society. I had often been seen in a sweat shirt. I been wearing the style since I was a kid, they had never been in fashion. I had been wearing mine because it made me feel comfortable it was grey I loved it. By the time I had stopped dreaming

or thinking about what clothing signifies what things you might be up to in your life a girl called Cathy joined me I could tell that Cathy was going to be a friend Cathy was younger than me about 10yrs I enjoyed talking to her very much. Cathy always went on about being a football manager I hope she makes its. She was a smoker too and always offered me cigarette I always said no and just laughed it off. Then there was Sam, Sam was the boss she knew everything about everything

Sam was the top cat Sam could pull you in and push you out. Sam was very clever. what I a liked about her the most was her style she had a lot of money that's why Sam drove two cars she had a company car to a Volvo convertible and Tm2. People about her were always thinking of her money. We all wished we had that kind of riches. I like cars to I had expensive tastes the cars I loved were super vehicles. Dave guru walked in as I walked out I need a cigarette. Dave the guru's stature as I remembered it 6,2 tall with a long uncut finger nails classy teenage jeans, and a mountaineering jacket he was about 46-59 and he looked like wolverine out of the comic book

I had heard him talk he had a quiet voice.

Then there was nick he was a busy fellow always doing something he was straight never drank did not smoke and often but butted into conversations satire was up right a very stern kind of character. I do not know how he got here but somebody was out to screw him up I could tell. He had that look of concern on his face. As soon as spoke he got up and adjusted his seat he did not sit down again but stood there talking. Dave guru was busy with his healing stone's. On the other side of the room he said in a soft voice "you're going to be aright" it was not if he could tell that I had a hundred problems. Everything stating that I had a hundred more. Once I had told him this he got up and walked away I hoped he would come back. The birds were noisy and the roads were getting noise.

Two men came out and walked right up to me and started talking about holy things they had to be mediators but I could not be sure then the girl came out. My lips were sealed I wanted to listen to the two chaps then Dave came out again I was beginning to think that Dave was an old busy body.

we had an interesting conversation, now the men were now talking about music or something I was sitting down I was not looking at anything or anybody I looked up again the guys were talking to me I did not even know they were trying to quiz my brain. The next thing that happened to me was that I was going to meet the man in charge he seemed nice enough we did not question each other two much for every one question he asked me I asked him double. He was convinced that I was crazy

there was a meeting in the shed, the shed room was going be

chapter34 The parcel

made an into a music room there was quite few musicians about me here too. I was convincing that I was in the right place. I had to tell the guys at home and Eugene I was ready to handle a relationship, although I was warned about making too many friends it had happened before when I was a teenager. I seemed to draw people to me I do not understand the actual power.

Girls was the subject I was no pimp or even considered myself a good lover but I could not get over the fact that I fancy every girl that I see, weather it was on the bus, in the high set, or the weather girl on to, whether it was rich, poor or if it had a good job or walked or drove whatever it was I was in love. Eugene knew it so did Dave and the guru said I well I will not repeat it, I on the other hand. I just thought of it as being sophisticated who wanted to be tied down. I did not fancy my new friends even though friends hit on friends the women in the Centre were a lot older than me. Then I saw an old friend she saw me first she says it couldn't have been more confusing conversation everything I said came out upside down in the end I got a slap in the face. I had to go home I left after saying good bye to everybody. I told them that I had to get back to do the gardening. The guru was the man he kept everything good the garden there was nothing wrong with the garden. Just before I left I got caught in an another conversation. I thought it was going to go on forever it was like a mothers meeting in here my mind thought. what's going on, I stared in amazement unable to speak and give an answer as the speaker was speaker was so fast. It's been a whole three minutes since you have closed your mouth I said I was watching a girl called Alison she shouted out and I am going to put this one out on you.

I left with the thought I did not understand her. Until she walked up to me and put her fag out on my jacket and just looked at me expecting a reaction but there was none. When I got home the paranoia hit me like a brick in the face. I tried talking to myself to make it go away. This was a feeling that I knew and it was not false to me. It was imposed on me by another man that I had met some time ago. if I remember he was an old house mate.

In the end the truth will come out whether I live or die I had not planned on dying yet exactly while I was still discussing my child hood with Cathy Ann and my consciousness or what was left of it as it had been ripped out of my brain. I looked down at the table I only did this when I did not want people to notice me I looked down at the pen also. Teaching and learning were the greatest gifts along with wisdom and love and peace. What was going to be my gift to mankind along with the gifts of speech we spoke about things which you could not maintain things like what was a thought, how many forms of communication' s was there how did languages come around and we discussed our own theory what is a normal thought if the thought is put in front of you then yes and if it's what you see then yes and where do your thought s go after you use them how many thoughts you would use in a life time I know I was correct and there was nobody to challenge me .

I looked over my shoulder Cathy was there Ann was talking to Alison.

When I got home I felt exhausted something was not quite right I felt a lot of emotion. I thought about it for a while maybe too much the tears filled my eyes I began to realize that it was the right thing to do.

There was a scuffle and the sound of feet coming down the hall way I pick up a cup of coffee which was sitting on the side it cold and properly been sitting there for days.

they both bundled in to my room hello then I knew that she was going to notice

"what's up".

there was a pause

"are you crying ".

"No of course not it's the coffee its hot", I put the cup up to my face to hide my tears again.

"Hi dude"

"hello guru"

It was Dave

He walked into the kitchen half asleep he was supposed to be taking an early night.

"Group hug".

they both stepped up and put their arms around me.

After five minutes they both cleared off shouting that it was good to have me back. I knew they were cool.

I was not bothered that I was drinking alcohol which I mistook for coffee all I was bothered about was covering my tears at that point in time.

The worst thing about me was that I could see things that were not really there I felt like I was being haunted and haunted by the things I could see I could not explain. The voices that I could see were not

real either they would come and go, and all they did is piss me off took another sip of the coffee which was whisky and spat it out instantly I had gone off the taste. A paranoid feeling came over me but this was a good paranoid feeling.

I looked up and scratched my head and the cook was just leaving I did not even know that I had a cook. He said good bye just as he was walking out he stopped. He was tall in stature short grey hair well-built body with skinny legs. He then began to question me because we had not met. In the end I finally convince him that I was his boss and he went home.

I was back in my house the voices were out amongst me and my mind they said that the sun will be out soon I replied "yes" but I thought for the first time why were they here by me, but it was all false the happy faces and the money. If these people really cared they would be up there but they were not, they were down here. In a way they were a compliment I was trying to look on the bright side of things but on the inside they were just like you and me ready to screw somebody over it was a well-kept secret until you knuckle down and wake up.

I walked into the lounge Dave was there on the phone it's your mum

"give me that" I snatched the phone from out of his hands. Which was out of character. He knew this and so did I. But he kind of just sighed away and I waved my hands franc ally to him sending him outside of the room. I was watching him as he slipped through the door. I then waved him back into the room.

there's a pause I handed the phone back covering the it so I could not be heard.

"wait" I said. " tell her I'm out doing the shopping".

"I heard that."

"mum".

she continued is everything alright.

The next journey was about to begin in time I was going to have some fun this time I was going to stand somehow it would make a difference I took off my jeans, pants, socks and t – shirt and put on the sun glasses this was new I knew that there was going to be a difference the sensation it was as if I was flying extremely fast rather than a floating driving feeling and I was able to see more it had widened my vision an extra 50%. I had entered a small room it was filled with old pitchers and paintings I had never been this far into or through my mind before. It reassembled a temple. On the other side of the room was filled with writing's and books

and all types of messages from writings in the past.

When I finally stopped looking around the thing that caught my eye's the most was the light it was pure black a lot darker than that I had ever experienced and a lot darker than I was previously used too.

I had got the sense that I was outside the color had changed again as I looked around. The light penetrated my back and went through down through my body and up to my brain. I was thinking that I was in the wrong place for a moment and I wanted to bring myself back. I was in an extremely large garden on what seemed to be an estate. The garden was vast rows and rows of trees. I wanted to walk back in so the light changed again I found myself walking through the large corridors in the mansion, it did not take me long to get used to the extremely large building

That's when I found a vault. I was thinking about what mum said

Chapter35 The next life

to me on the phone but that kind of surpass as I had found the vault. I grabbed the vault wheel and turned it span uncontrollable until it stopped the vault was too hard for me to open it by myself I was just about to give up when I heard a voice say "open it with your mind".

I closed my eyes and used the thought it was done. I could hear my mum as well. Mum always said you don't get something for nothing you get something for something. Inside the vault was money I stood there for a moment there must have been millions and millions in there it was everywhere stacked high to the celling I was not going to touch it I was not a theft that was not why I was making these journeys into my mind I wanted to learn and explore I had enough money of mine own besides how would I bring it back. I stood there for ages thinking how I could shift it.

I closed the vault and went back outside, it began to rain I could see the rain drops falling on the floor and the sound of the pitter patter was getting launder and launder, the voices were busy discussing why I had not taken the

138

there was no point it was not going anywhere and I knew I could find it at any time. There was the subject of peace something that the human mind in the modern world should try to accomplish maybe I could take the money and use it. I went back into the mansion and entered the dining room. The meditation was for me was so addictive every time I made my way back I would feel sick you know cold sweats sleepless nights aching back I made my way back through my mind. I was busy now I had forgotten who I was all I could think about was winning my soul back. It was going to be a huge battle. I could imagine it could be like a war. On the way back I met the old man again Dave I was beginning to believe that he was not a real threat but I found him really annoying although

 I kept on seeing him around me on a number of occasions I just did not want to mansion him he was just beginning to get inside my head.

It was funny just a second ago I saw a friend he stopped me and asked me for a cigar he had questions. It was kind of like a mind check just to see if anybody experience the same as me. Anew saints and a couple of priests, the whole of the church I do not know who else comes into mind. I began to see that somebody was going out of there way the better my mind. Well a point taken I am wanted was the thought I know now that I am a wanted man and I know when I am not wanted, and I know that I want in a different way. I am one.

Gary walked in and old friend hello I said greeting him. He was a care taker and was really friendly he was tall and worn he wore an old jumper the typical type of clothing that a hobo would wear blue trousers, suit jacket and grey jumper. I did not look up this time I looked down. Something suspicious was occurring around my thoughts what I looked forwards and down at his feet, my head was firmly in motion of facing down and in the background I could hear a cup of tea being made the echo of the spoon being steed around the cup echoed right into my brain. I could hear another friend walking in it was Shaun and other members talking behind me, the radio was playing it was as if everything had been slowed down. Somebody slams a door. The conversation that had started was of discomfort. I on the other hand had been cursed from the very bones of my feet to my head. I was being pestered by a girl because I loved another. That's the reason why I was there, I had caused jealously and believed that my love for her was a curse. There were some children around me and the other members. I tried deeply to look happy. If they were children like myself I asked myself how would it be accursing I asked myself again there was no answer and I thought about it hard. I had over spoken when a rush of thoughts reached my mouth and not my mind.

I was standing inside by a door now and I was in the way I tried to move into space but more and more members would walk in. Another and another and another then that's when I saw her. I had never seen anybody like it before. She had dark brown hair and her plain face reminded me of my mother. This was the second time I had meet like this it was a perfect look. I looked away so that she would not notice me when I looked up again she was making her way to the fire exit. That's when a shimmering light came over me it was most overwhelming then Gary walked by a gave me a nudge and a wink.

All the doors of the building were open in the building and that's when I heard it I couldn't

believe it I could hear this squeaking voice I was too shy to answer it let alone understood it. It was something that I could not comprehend why me. After all the people who I stopped in the street and all the people that I had meet at this Centre I was still the only person who could see and hear. The things that only a crazy even person would see maybe I was crazy but could not see it. I shouted by mistake it just came out I wanted to know why. Was it something that I had done, or was it something that I had heard or was it something that I had read. Surly meditation could not cause these kind of symptoms. And if it did why was not I warned about this. The next stop was the bus stop it was still raining I was soaked right through I tried to dry myself off with my jacket, it worked for a little while. To walk was not that bad thing considering the weather I was got off the bus to walk home alone but it was only a short distance I did this on my own quite happily, I was quite paranoid at one part of the journey. On my way home I saw Gary on his bike he was racing it the roaring of the engine bike was ripping my ears apart but only for a few seconds. We were good friends but we kept silent. Sometimes silence is the best relationship. To be honest we hardly said a word to each other it was like we were telepaths or something. All we would do was look at each other and we would make each other laugh. Laughter was good I think we laughed for around Five minutes last time we spoke. We laughed over anything and everything. I was timing it on the clock the clock was on the wall in front of me in fact it when I looked at it I was sure that it was telling the right time but at the second glance it was wrong. I looked at my watch I was right it was wrong. That's when I realized that I was going to miss my bus when I got to the Centre. I knocked on the door.

I had just made it home and to my surprise everybody was out. I knew there was something wrong nobody had left me the key although I had already had one. But it was not for this lock. This had occurred more than once this was the third time this week.

It was getting cloudy outside; it began to rain I stood next to the back door. perched under the ledge of the back door hoping that the weather would not get any worse. The house that I was resting upon was an old restaurant it was converted to a six-bedroom Victorian mansion it had a huge garden. I remembered when I was young I would play here for hours outside in the sunshine but it was raining outside now if I could dance it would bring the sun out. The rain was slowing down slowly pouring out of the of the over filled gutters onto the patio flooring. I closed my eyes.

Shaun and I knew the girl she came out with all smiles again. The traffic in the background slowly became silent. Ann and Sarah walked towards me we were all by the bus stop. A bus pulled over Gary was next to it on his bike clumsy revved his engine, Sarah busts out laughing she says to Ann that it was funny, another lady walked past the bus shelter She was old and looked worn she had her hands full of shopping bags we should have helped her. A few minutes later Sarah's bus turns up. It all went quiet that's when a loud voice shouted out that's my stop.

Your supposed to push the button when your bus stop comes near.

What button, what stop.

That was tough luck she had missed her stop and in saying that it the smile of her face slowly dropped into a sad look. The bus turned up and we all got on it. Ann did not say anything she just lit up another cigarette. We asked her to put it out as we were on public transport. She ignored the fact and continued to puff it even worse when she had finished she stubbed it out on the bus floor. Not that it meant anything but a pour attitude. She did not know at the time but you only get one chance in my book.

I was slowly hoping that the keys to my mansion would arrive, the Post man was supposed to bring to me this morning. It was a new mansion a little different to my other mansion in town. To be honest this was more like a winter retreat. I did not visit the mansion enough to call it home. I had put the keys into a parcel knowing that I was going to be here at the mansion in the morning ready to meet the postman. The rain slowly stopped but in a few minutes started again. All I wanted to do was get out the

chapter36 Anybody for tea

cold and into the warm.

I questioned the question.

The roses in the garden looked good they were at full bloom there was lots of flowers in my garden I planted most of them myself, mind you in saying that there was one road cone, a skip, large pine tree, some benches to sit on. I could see all the way to the drop in Centre through my mind, and I could visualize the people, the parked cars, the inside of the old buildings which was a children's home before the celling, and floors everything the stairways and last of all the art the pitchers on the walls I could also see the blind, the dead and the dumb. I closed my eyes and brought myself back. Meditating outside seemed rather peaceful but not that exciting.

I was sitting in my bed room the doors and windows were closed and I think the bedroom door was locked I had some music on nothing special just an old cd.

I took a large mouth full of water out of a large glass which was sitting on the bedroom side board I could see the little droplets of water left over at the bottom of the glass. It must have been hot outside but as I recall in the visions it was always raining. I put the glass down wiped my mouth and slowly closed my eyes.

This was great I had never been to top of a mountain before and this mountain was the biggest that I could ever image I checked my ruck sack what I had in it. There was water, a blanket, a pair of shoes, a jacket, some food and a pair of gloves. it seemed so similar the paths like old trails something that I seemed to recognize. It was built into my mind kind of like a bird before it can fly it knows itself what its wings are for and it will throw itself out of its nest to achieve this so I believe that this journey is already mapped out in my brains so that I could see this vision. So up the mountain I walked I knew that I was walking in the right direction and before I knew it I was meeting other walkers, A young man caught my eyes. I knew him he seemed familiar I had never meet anybody with his statue and posture he was quite short he was still a boy. There was a girl as well I could just about see her she was right at the front. I could not reach her so I called out her but she never heard.

It was still raining it seemed to rain wherever I went. In fact, I checked the weather by mobile phone I was glad it worked and had not run out of power. They said there was going to be sunshine what I got was far from it. I looked down at my hands and thought that they looked weird. There was something wrong with them I could feel something there was quite a lot wrong with me. When I looked at my hands I got the notion to think about the sides of

my head which I could not do without thinking about my eyes. I tried to think about my feet but that was impossible too. By the time that I had finished looking at my feet I decided to look at the rest of me

body I looked up, down, left and right. It was time for me to leave to the mountain. I said good bye to the other walkers and left. When I got back the next day I went straight to the drop in Centre. In the car park was Sarah, an, and Gary. It was late around 12 o'clock.

The next place that I was to journey was to the bus stop again I had got on the bus

which was heading for the town, on the journey I had met another girl her name was Alex she was becoming a friend closer than any of my spiritual lovers, brothers, and sisters. she was skinny I did not have an issue with that. I looked out of the window. What did I notice about the outside it had become of less green there was sometimes a lot of green but it looked out of place it seemed to me that the whole planet was made of concrete pathways and dead trees and now I did not hear anybody say or mention their name's? It was concrete. I was not trying change the planet, I looked again and again and again and it was true Alex was true all I could see was concrete the roads and houses.

 I kind of lost my temper a bit and spoke out loud this caused a fight. with myself and Alex a verbal disagreement. Then my bus slowly entered the country side the passengers were getting more and more restless the smaller children on the bus started to bicker and crying came afterwards. The noise was unbearable but I had to laugh it off. It was not surprising that a fight broke out between two of the teenagers as it happens I was there to settle them down, it's always me I said to myself. I grabbed the first teenager who was really kicking off and told him to shut his mouth and sit down he did it staight away the other boy continued and was literally in tears. Then for no reason a girl in the back ground broke down and started crying too, nobody went to comfort her. It came to the point when just about everyone on the bus had tears in their eyes or was fully crying. I guess the experience was too much for her. When I looked around and down I found myself on a bed with her. I was sitting on my bed legs stretched and crossed over. She was sitting the same legs crossed over and looked in deep meditation. I do not know if she was in deep meditation with style I did not ask her or try to wake her. I know now that I was not the only human who could know everything about everything and through my experiences. I was not going to share my experiences I was not going to doctors and I kept a clear view of what I was experiencing I was not about to give up. I sat down on my mat I closed my eyes I found out that the girl was extremely close to me it was the select the elite that I was coming to the conclusion that I must find a way of telling my soul the truth. That that I was dying that there was a conspiracy to murder me out of the circle which I had created. The cat, the present dent, my other self, they were all suspects in my mind oh yes and my flat mates, I could quite easily be on my own but I wanted to be with my friend. A reunion was what I had in mind a meeting of old friends and pals that I met on my journey that I had met through meditation through my mind. Many people say that the mind is a beautiful and great minds think alike. I was sure as hell not going to die and I made it clear to those who were following me.

I knew something was going on but I just chose to ignore it. But my wife who was a gambler and was bent and was trying to murder me. We fell out over gambling debt she sold my car to pay for it without my permission. She tried to approach me on several occasions she would do things like slipping a tea bags into my dinner that she cooked hoping that I would swallow it and choke to my death, but I knew there was a tea bag in it but I said nothing as it was petty I was not going to make a big fuss over it she only used to have dreams of murder me. I could hear her in her sleep talking about it. I opened my eyes I could feel a presents I did not want to say a thing but it was a friend of a friend's dad. I tried to stop him but he was too powerful I was now using the words of wisdom and then a long prey. But he still persisted on entering my mind. He had my soul I had no choice but to talk to him. He was persistent in sucking the soul out of my mind. I tried to ween him off me but it was too late he was in my head.

Going back to my first premonitions of myself in the smokers hut I had to ask myself what was I doing there. The day had been long I had obverse everything that happened on that day, in that dream or meditation, meaning the vision of the vision of what you begin to visualize once you have found your destination or place of rest. In meditation the word merit was just made up so that it was easier for its players to remember. The names of places your soul went to visit, Then the little girl in the corner of my room said something to me it was so soft I could just about hear her. I asked her if she could repeat it again but she said it was too hard. She looked frighten by my approach. So I asked her if she was in danger she said no, I am not in fact that's when she said that it was pure sunlight she was after that's when her tone changed I knew it from somewhere It was my mother. So I asked the girl if she knew who she was there was silent for a minute or too. And then we both said together son she went on, so there I was a 38 yr. old man with a teenage mum how did that work out. I began to talk to her it was so real the more I spoke the more she laughed out loud and louder it lasted almost 5 minutes and it seemed like hours. Then time ran out and I had to return myself to myself.

All my friends had gone home I had travelled to three or four destinations in and through my meditations. I had only just met my mentor who was a teenage girl who happened to be me

mother in her next life. So I had to ask myself where was my father. I had asked that question before, she walked around the

chapter37 closed subject

room for a while then went to the window she was persistent in trying to change the subject her words were stuttered she became quite upset, I did not blame her. She them caught her breath after wiping the tears off her face. She tried to explain that my father could not be found and he was not from this planet and for a very long time she did not speak with him. I found the conversation upsetting and I did not understand it until she said he would join us soon but she never said that if he did not finish his mission he would miss the opportunity. She said he would join us in the next haven and not in this one. Right from the beginning I knew that what I was doing I was controlling myself through different parts of the spiritual journey which would be the beginning of my next life I was not going to die this was merely the start of a new life I wanted to come back as me well what I mean is I would be me but I would have a new body I don't think I would come back as a new born but I always believed I would come back as a teenager tiresome, bad timing but witty. When I realized I had found a new body I am slightly going out of my depths here but I will continue I wanted to destroy it I could see what I was doing to myself was bad but I knew it felt good. I just said to myself but I had to have one more try I was stupid I knew that I was dead now God had explained everything he said that I was so good that he had to keep on redirecting me and this was my fifty forth resurrection I had or was finished working in haven it was only that I would have approach the main man himself and ask him if I could be resurrected as my actual self and try to make all the decisions myself. That I would put all the wrongs I did right and perfect my life so that one day I would live in heven again. It's all complicated I do not expect you to understand it. So back to the journey of being me. I could feel my body, it was toned to perfection I could feel my stomach it was muscular and my legs were well built too. The only problem I had was the first problem of the rest of my life again it was perfect I was being contacted and I knew straight away it was God he had decided to talk with me. He said he was leaving that he had had enough of the human race but we were not to be blamed for things like wars and global warming because it was all him he was behind it. I asked him by bowing my head while kneeling and saying nothing where to His reply at first was that he gave me an overwhelming stare his eyes that got bigger, I'm moving to the artic he said the polar bear needs me. Is there anything else I said what do you what me to do I said it was sad I could feel the tears build up in my eyes I did not want to think about it in fact I just manage to get a hold of myself. For a long time, all I could think about was happy thoughts but something had come over me. While I was going through this slight transformation I looked up in front of me still bowed down to the Gods the big eyes which he had and as he raised up his arms in greatness he had on a big apparel, white and he appeared to be holding a wooden staff he was doing something to my soul. He gave an almighty tap of his staff onto the floor and my soul was raised up. And was filled with pure light with an another tap of his staff he filled me with all the knowledge of kingdoms of heaven and the earth. God had to change his clothes. I suggested a shirt and jeans he took off his white appeal and changed behind his throne he was talking to me as he changed. He had finished and said if I would not mind if he wore a sweat shirt rather than a shirt as was a little bit childish. I smiled and said that's fine. He bowed down and sucked his face in. I Really wanted to go with him. But my job now was to rule over the heavens. God past his staff to me and put a baseball cap on his head. Then he disappeared I did not see him go and I had to double check. In my new body I had only sat down for a second a few minutes just to give myself a taster. I could have glided away I wanted to move fast I had a lot to offer and I had a lot of ideas. I was in me knew body and I could feel my mind It was full again. I sat down in the position head up legs crossed. I found myself moving through my mind extremely fast it less than a spilt second and I also found that I could find anything whether it was an object or a human being. I had not been experimenting with my new mind for too long before I found her it was a little girl something had

happened it was her mum she could not find her I said to the girl I would find her for her and I did she said thank you and clasped my hand.

All my friends had gone and I was the only one left I had travelled to three or four destinations in and through my meditations. I had only just met the girl was the reincarnation of my mother who incidentally was still alive. So I had to ask myself where was my father and what about if I was the only child I did not recall having brothers or sisters. Thinking about this made me feel upset. And after a while I had begun to cry I wiped the tears from my eyes with a hanky. The night was young and the could were apart in the sky the sun was slowly setting and it looked beautiful on the sunset. I had not been here on the planet for long I did not understand it until I heard a whisper in my left ear you have not finished your mission so you cannot join us at this particular moment then the voice said you can join us in the next haven or on earth the priests said. Right from the start I knew that I was controlling myself through the havens and stars hoping to find the ultimate journey, the buzz, the rush of the best spiritual journey which would be the beginning, the next life. I had not died I had merely continued my life elsewhere. In my new body, I had only sat down for a minute just to give myself a taster I could have glided myself straight in to heaven it's self but I did not want to rush things, I had other ideas.

The first person who I wanted to meet was the girl who was my mother. I was very eager to meet her so I sat down and crossed my legs. In me knew body as I did was filled with pure light and only to my surprise I found out that it was not my mum but it was her house which I was giving high praises too. In my mind or in that house something had happened. The little girl had gone also I could not find her. So I waited and I waited but nothing. I remember the things that she had told me, I was upset that I had only met with her once. I was on a journey I knew inside that I was beginning to find my actual self; I think that's what you would call it. If you were going to experience anything that I had experienced in the last four years or so that it reminds me to tell you of these assurances, it did not happen overnight. I was getting closer to my destination as the time slowly past that when I got a message the same voice in the same ear like a soft breeze tickling my sides. I was going to meet my father and as a teenager I was surprised that I could not speak with them both together. It all came down to this conclusion I had to figure out this predicament I had met my mother on a plain when she was a little girl and I met my grown up father in an another life as a teenager, but I had no mum as a teenager and why could not find my father on this plane. I did not want to bother myself with the thought. It was clearly a sore point.

After we had played together we sat down both in my vision I politely asked him for a drink then I realized that it he was a she the only reason that I thought this was because she was a man was both woman and men wear the same white apparel. So I sat down on their plane, they had made sure that I was made welcome they showed me in gifts they had some and now had some. I wondered around for a while I felt quite lost. I had not traveled this far out of my mind before and I think I lost my way abet. I did not want to tell anybody about but with the amount of meditation that I had done I should have been able to find my way back. I found it a little bit embarrassing. That's when I had a vision so powerful that if I had spoken about it would have upset the heavens. The vision was of a past life it was my life actual somebody had attempted to murder me it was only a small vision but its power was fouth score. That was the thought. I have never forgotten the feeling of being hurt and feeling hurt in just one moment in all my life. And I was sickened by this. And from that day I asked the lord to stay by my side. I was getting tired then out of the corner of my eye I saw a lonely figure it was coauthoring around it was in hell. I came across as friendly but I had to many problems the girl who has no name looks at things in an over serious way. She says that she is a friend through all the meditations that I have done I could sincerely say that she has a problem excepting herself and the truth. What was the TRUTH. I know after experiencing this the truth had died. Saying the word truth was reminding of the little girl I met and it was filling her without light. I could see her standing there

I did not want to disturb her so I got down on one knee and said a prayer wishing her the best of luck. That's when I realized that I had to get knack to normal life. It had been four years since I had left my consciousness we had travelled through the eye to many places.

The scariest Australia, the most loved in England, The most fear some of the plans of Africa on to the continent of America. That was where my family was all the knowledge sucked into me. The father I travelled the more gained knowledge I have travelled across the earth and universe with the four highest heavenly beings which God has sent me. Saints, angels, brothers and princes they have all been my guides and my friends. When I awoke I found myself in my bed there were some people standing by the bed they were all nattering. I looked around the room I could clearly see that I was being spoken to by some very important people I could see two men they were tall and they lent over me they introduced themselves as the two kings there was a little boy he announced himself as the prince. There was a short silence then the boy prince spoke "we have become great friends they commanded",

My opinion always varied but to them was valued. They explained that they had been there all of the time. And that they had been travelling with me from the start of my meditations. They said that they had been watching over me. That was the end of the adventure and a new adventure was about to arise. This time it began with my pen, I picked it up and started writing I was writing about everything which I had experienced

the words were just flowing out of me it was like a water fall of words which echoed around me I was excited. First of all, I thought my writing was rubbish for some time but it all made sense in the first place. I had to write about healing and mediation. It was not impossible to turn off the mind, I've seen it done. It takes a tablet or two but it works.

At last I was being to see it was the fifth year all was well there was one place which I wanted to see desperately and that was the underneath of the ocean. What was down there I asked myself. I took the matter up with the princess her answer to that was well we do own the oceans as well. I aged but I knew that GOD would take the Oceans back.

The princess asked me if I was ready I replied yes she took my hand and in a split second we were there in under the sea. I can explain the feeling that I was experiencing the water was warm the water ran fast it rushed past me as I was hit by some

turbulence. For a moment I had lost her visually as I was being swept away the water began to drag us apart, For the next couple of minutes I stayed in deep meditation it seemed like hours.

When I had finished I the princess asked me if she I would like to join her for dinner as I began to eat I had reason to believe that I had be here before. Everything I did was the same the smell and the taste of the air. Everything that the princess spoke of was connecting me to her world, I was connected her word. H err words echoed through the dining room as we spoke.

It was late winter when I finally had the pleasure of asking her for her hand I proposed to her in front of everybody to make sure she could not say no. I was wrong her declined a few more months went by and I asked her again and her answer was the same again no. The asking went on and on I was not going to give up. My politeness and my dress changed and I went from being polite to being rude. From being quiet at the dining table to bellowing crude jokes. I made sure that I would always bump into in corridors and apologies and cheeky conversations while she was bathing just to get a peak of her and other things like that eventually NY the time summer had come she had changed her mind. I had convinced her finally she agreed to marry me. I was delighted to experience the same. On the contrary I saw everything that you experienced and you were by my side. She replied. And the brothers about us agreed also, I still could not believe it was like everything was falling back into place. I watched out for accessibly I already knew that she was my wife and I was married to her. Because I have the qualities I was quite forgiving and I had good qualifications. I suppose you could say that about anybody but these were not ordinary people. As time the people only chose to meet on planes. As we grew apart our love for each other grew stronger and stronger until it had bonded and tied itself back together.

For the power and love our lord God had given you and me was no mistake. It was so powerful that God himself had to bless it and enter the spirit, he was blessing the planet and the solar system. They needed a new name for planet earth. The earth was growing   and its name was undecided. Everything was well I stood up I ached all over my body I had lost a considerable amount of weight. I hobbled off to kitchen. The pain grew quickly. It had started in my legs and ran up through me to my body then I reached my face finally. I began to cry; my tears were not like normal tears I had big tears. I was saddening we all were. I could still see a few things. The expression on my face as I was told was sort of happy and then sad and looked as if I was going to laugh. The pain eventually subsided and the feelings in my body went back too normal. I was seeing things made of pure light, and blue. What I was going to experience next was the knight hood I was given three gifts the first was my mediation and imagination. But Before I was given the knight hood I had to pick a quarrel with the king and queen to see if I was holy enough I lost I was beaten by my wife and the king and queen but my wife stood by me. We had shared quite a lot since we had met we had even cried together once or twice she never lost her temper as I showed her my emotions as she showed me hers, I got down on my knees and said a prey. I filled my eyes with light and my soul came back to me it was something that I worried about the most, my meditation even though now I was getting good at it I still made mistakes it was like a job interview you do not open your mouth until you are asked the questions in my case I was a bit hasty and wanted to know everything in such a short period of time it's like your dinner you eat it very slowly even if you have not got a lot. To me it was like time travel I could be near or far away and think nothing of it although I tended to stick to the same places going back and forth depending on how far I had walked on that day. Meditation became my life even more so I had prey. I would just sit there and prey all day long forgetting now actually how dangerous it could be but I kept a limit on things, or I would simply meditate. Prey brought me excitement and took me to places I did not know a lot about prey but it kept my soul contempt with everything. The hardest thing possible about all of this was how I was going to keep the peace it was an ongoing trust a pact between myself and God and I choose to keep it with him. I had been summoned to the throne I knew that the king wanted to test me I walked in I felt a cold breeze the hair stood up on my neck with excitement.

bow your head I was given a nudge and prompted so I did so. I said it although I was not asked a question I was about to say to the question but the true answer was yes I wanted the crown I could not help myself after a long period of thought I was beginning to think about writing some of my experiences down so I did it I wrote the book. The book sold about half a million copies on the first day I was rich it explained everything that I experienced in this book. At the end of my journeys I met with my brother we sat and discussed just about everything that there

was to discuss the evening ended with a cup of tea. I had not seen her for about three months. In the morning it was a usual routine for me down to the bus stop, I grabbed what I could hoping that I would miss my house mates and my brother s early morning banter about me being lazy. I began to think about how all this meditation started.

If I was not so popular my best friends would have not tried to remove me but they tried and they tried real hard living without my spirit was quite hard some people say the spirit is murderous other say you need to feel the spirit it exists around you and in you. My wife knew me well by now and she invited me outside to watch the sunset. It was extremely tranquil blue. In the olden days the sun would have been a bright yellow color and the set a crimson red. Talking about the sun made me think of the

ink of the last part of the story. Everybody was in place we were all sitting in the dining area there was a large white table with large clear glasses it was quite a shock when I found out what they were serving. There were three plates in front of me. On the plate was a meal, it was in two special tablets and there was a knife and a fork I sat at one end of the table with my wife the princess at the other I leant over the speaker to so I could press the button to speak to her.

"is this it."

she replied "just eat it please."

I said nothing the tablets were quite hard and large it was green and white. It was a capsule. I dabbled with it on my plate with my knife and fork. I could not cut the food in half, so I swallowed it whole. There was nothing for a minute or two then the strangest tastes came to my mouth it was stupendously delicious in fact it was fantastic, fabulous and delightful.

"it's great I said.

That was the last time I saw the princess. I had finally awoken Dave was standing over me "yes he is back you've been out for a quite a while I vet got all of your messages your agents been worried sick you have got a tone

of mail oh yes you got the lead part in the film you were talking about".
I answered him quaintly "well I am the best go on clap and applauded".

"you don't look too happy".

"No I mean yes I'm over the moon".

"you start tomorrow evening".

The next day came around quickly I had no time to prepare myself for the part, which in my case was frustrating I explained the problem to Dave as I went through the script. I managed to pick up the first four parts. I spoke to my agent we agreed that I should just make the rest up and hoped that the director would except whatever came out of my mouth. I was pretty good at my job I could hit a scene with one to three lines in a second so making the rest of the script up would not be a problem. Well it was time to go to the set. Dave was driving me there we got into the car he asked me if I had everything. Pops I have forgotten the script. We went back inside I had left it on the kitchen side I pick it up it was as heavy as the bible and as thick as the works of Shakespeare. We go back into the car, he asked me what time we had to be there I think my agent said ten a clock what's the time he did not answer me straight away. We won't be late I know a short cut to the studio we will miss the morning traffic. I did not reply. There was a short silence I asked Dave if he would put the car radio on he said yes on with the music, so we started the journey I felt kind of dreamy everything I looked at seem not real the scenery looked false like it was fake and I felt a weird feeling a good weird feeling there was a tingling in my feet and then it went straight up to my arm. Break a leg that's the spirit that's what I thought it was good luck to say that. I looked out of the window it was I would say different I was watching the people walk by some of them looked pour others looked rich I was pretty rich and I was thankful. It just made you think about the divide in society I was so glade I was not pour. I did not want to close my eyes I did not want to miss a thing I was taking everything in. people, cars, old biddy's, women everything that I saw I was thankful for. Dave was not speaking which was not unusual, he was concentrating on the journey, he was a good driver and fast to. He loved his car in fact as I thought of this he just put the foot down I opened the window and stuck out my head just to humor Dave. He drove one handed at about ninety miles' amour he lent his arm outside of the window like and LA gangster I think he did that because it was the cool way to drive. We pulled up to the traffic lights Dave slowly revved up the engine one minute and we were off again.

"Do you know where you are going".

"yeah I think so take a left at the bride groom shop I mean the wedding shop".

"Are yeah I've got you". He replied.

We were there Dave pulled up into the car park there was at least a hundred cars parked here there was no spaces I told Dave after looking for a space to just pull up right outside the main entrance, he did so.

We walked inside, it was like a cheap frill nobody recognized me. I understood this was not going to be a low budget film. After about twenty minutes of greeting people. And meeting people. I met my agent and I was taken for the press review. This was brill we sat there at a table the cameras streaming all over the place I walked in and sat down There was a glass of water waiting for me I sat down and met the rest of the cast. The camera's started it was amazing I did not have to say a word. Clicking and the flashing of the camera lights was all I could see. That lasted for about ten minutes then there was silence that's when the press asked the first question. It was not for me the question but I answerd it anyway the guy next to me gave me a nudge I then realized what I had done and apologized the camera kept on clicking away. I was given a chance to speak eventually

my voice was a little squeaky so I adjusted my throat and answered the question I could not believe it. I wiped the sweat from my brow it had run into my eyes so I had begun to squint I went for a glass of water but due to not being able to see because of the sweat in my eyes I spilt it all over the actor next to me he grunted and shouted what the hell do you think I was doing. I went to stand up as I did I caught the table cloth and pulled half of and what was on the table in front of me on to my lap and the floor. The camera clicked even more, I was busy apologizing the other actors and started laughing. It was quite funny I guess I then on purposely fell on the floor and quickly got up there was a cheer I took a bow and then poured myself another drink of water. Well that was the end of that the camera men slowly left I and was left alone the filming was going to start in a day or two I had accommodation at the studio. Me and Dave wanted to find the set, the studios were massive they had everything it was not as big as universal or warner brothers I would say it around or a bit bigger than pinewood studios. It did not take us long to find it was large. The set was massive everything was enlarged to fit the camera' s. I was looking for a chair with my name on it. When I found it I smiled it was a large director's chair it had my name on the back I jumped into it. Dave was busy taking photographs of set. I closed my eye s it felt high up and it held my weight I was only around thirteen stone I was wondering when the rest of the crew would turn up it was going to be a couple of hard nights and busy mornings. Dave had taken his last picture which was of me in the chair. Then he left I was on my own it was peaceful. I could smell the air it was sweet and somebody had left a bouquet of flower s and a bottle of beer for me. In the bouquet was a greeting card there was a message it read all the best break a leg and there was some lavender. Underneath the flowers was a box of chocolates. I did not open them or the bottle of beer although as I felt fine it gave me something to focus on the next morning I awoke to the sound of a truck and the director's car had also pulled up the other members of the cast had just awoken it was funny but everybody turned up at the same time. I did not see the win bagel last night but there was three of them one of them was mine. The director was an odd looking fellow he was wearing a big jacket with shorts and sandals. I introduced myself his reply to my introduction was yes I know who you are this guy would set me on fire it was not going to be easy working for him I had now taken this into account. It was a dog eat dog world and he was the Rottweiler and I was the chewawa. I picked up the bottle beer opened it and took a sip a big sip. The director was getting his stuff together. He called out I want everybody on the set in fifteen. He meant fifteen minutes I closed my eye' s once more too ready myself. I put the bottle down on the table the other actors turned up and got into their seats two minutes later the whole crew had turned out. The crew was massive there was people everywhere. The adrenaline pumped through my body. I was all sweaty I wiped my brow I was pretty fit the sun was just coming out and the dew on the ground was rising into air making a soft fog. I came over light headed that was the beer I was a light weight.

The filming had begun there was silent not a sound was to be made it was so quiet I could hear my self breathe I had the main role but I was not introduced into the film until the third scene. The filming went on it was almost tiring just watching it the cast that I was working with were right armatures the first guy who's name I can't recall had a stutter it was half a day gone before

he had captured his style and it took eighteen takes I could see the rest of the cast doing the same. I was not board but I could not bear to watch this pour guy any more I went off the set to find my win bagel.

It took me five minutes to find it and about half an hour to figure out where the keys were to get in. They were underneath the box of chocolates which were left for me with another note it read have a smashing day and best of luck and break a leg. It was not signed. I let myself in, it was quite spacious it had everything laptop, TV, Games console. and the kitchen was stacked with beer, wine and food in the fridge was milk and cheese. Great I thought. I wanted to meditate but I decided not to matter of principal never mix work with pleasure. I turned on the game's console this was unreal the computer game was the film that I was staring in I had to ask myself the question when was the script written because it was a computer game as well. I was never any good at games so I just grabbed myself a beer and sat down on the sofa and put my feet up on the table casually. I did not feel tired but I just felt that I should go to sleep the armature actors were going to take all day I could tell. It was hot for one and two I wanted another beer and I wanted to crash out. I was on the bed for about five say ten minutes tossing and turning I could not sleep it was too hot for one and two I was too excited I got up and went for a walk. I got up and walked out of the win bagel I left the door open. The film studio was huge I did not know where to start not the pub and there was one I could have gone to the theme park it seemed fun enough but I did not fancy it. I breathed the fresh air into my mouth and exhaled the freshness of the air cleansed my soul. The fog had disappeared and it looked like it was going to be a nice day but just as I said this to my self the sun went in and it came over cloudy this always happens to me. I took my mobile phone out of my jacket pocket and checked the weather report that was funny according to the weather report on my phone it's going to be sunny all day.

You can never believe the weather report I guess. I made it back to the main set, the director had just finished giving the actor his directions his loud voice had an echo to it he demanded that there was quiet on the set just like all directors do. I made it to my chair I picked up the bottle of beer which was open and sipped from. And watched. It was going to be a long day I could tell. Then out of the blue I got a text it was Eugene the text which is a message electronically sent through to you via your phone said best of luck and break a leg kiss kiss kiss that made my day I texted her back straight away. I wrote, Hello babe having a great time but these Actors are armature. She texted me back almost straight away.

I had I've got his car, house, oil, everything he was some flash dummy from America.

He had a pair of eights I had nothing, he thought something and he folded.,"

"Well you'll the promotions around twenty million

"that's a hell of a lot of loot, I'm your best friend."

"I know".

"Know I mean it".

"Eugene made five hundred thousand on the cat walk Yesterday she got a check and on top of that she got another three hundred thousand for the movie".

"I on the other hand made seven and a half million on a game of blackjack I bluffed my way right from the start

you look good".

"Okay that's enough about money".

"Well that's all good news what's on the TV" this morning, we laughed, cried and eventually went to bed.

The next morning, I walked into the living room

"what's going on here."

"hay "

"hi".

I jumped into the arm chair it was my chair. It was my chair and nobody sat in my chair it was house rules.

And the second was that nobody disturbs me while the footballs on.

"well" I said, there was a pause "how is everybody".

"so Dave how did it really go".

"It went really well how much did you really make?".

"After tax and Agents fees".

"obviously"

"Sorry I cannot tell you it is not that I do not want to tell you it is too hard to account after all the promotions and TV. The film its self-will properly makes a hundred million in the next year".

I was the lead.

It would have been really good if Eugene could have known my child, any way I Had to get home there was something that I had to do I had to spend more time with Dave and Eugene or they would suspect something. So we spent a few more days loving the house which I was trying to sell my mum came over to she was a funny old lady all I kept on saying is as a joke was how does she like her tea she never caught on. It was Wednesday I told the others that I had had enough over a game of twister you know that old on the floor board game I walked trying to look necked as If I was about to pass out to my bedroom. I thought that they had sassed me out when I was called back but I politely declined. If they found out that all I did was sleep all day I mean how much sleep does the actor need.

I transcended back into the journey it was colorful there was a huge forest that kept on coming into my mind me and the princess had spoken about it. I wanted to be with her all the time I was in love with her just her appearance and she was always polite to her people she was a giver of life like a water fall forever flowing with knowledge she was forgiving we had often spoke about bathing there, there was a river close by.

I had just a woke I was woken by the TV it took me a few second s to gather my soul and mind I got up and got dressed I put on a shirt which I left untucked, a jumper, briefs, socks and jeans in that order, I stood by my bedroom window for a minute.

Everybody was in the great hall in the palace that's all I could see it was like being famous twice over once on the earth and the second on the plane. The Cat had the camera and it was taking pitchers of all the people who were dancing, cheering and clapping. You name it, it was a great celebration. There were all kinds of kind people here in the palace. I was about to take my eye off the Cat when I looked up all I could see was the president and 23 stuffing their faces. The food was of the highest quality although it was very small in stature as you already know. There were children running everywhere in the hall ways and jesters juggling.

On the next day I awoke in her arms half a sleep on the dining table I was still in the the palace. Eugene I had thought of her for the first time I had crated this all of this by chance it was the first time that I thought of inviting my friends into my world, there was no way I was going to give them up.

The president was there he said to me look at this letter again please, the message had changed he asked if it was my doing. 23 returned my job to me. It was like I had become extremely powerful and it was said that I was a teacher and should be watched day and night.

In the next days the Cat had tried to befriend me again for the second time he claimed was just being a Cat and he said that he desperate to get his body back. He was searching for a body like mine. He laughed a lot while we spoke about this it was properly true but I have my doubts.

Although I thought that everything was going good all the time my luck was about to change it started first thing in the next morning I had a letter. The postman came up to the door he

knocked loudly and waited. I was a bit slow to answer the door I had a letter it was marked special delivery. I just caught him as he was just turning away.

"Hi there how are you doing "I put my American accent just to impress him.

"your mail". he said.

"Cheers have a nice day". I replied I was in a rush to open it the envelope I mean in it was the letter. Ripping it open I found a letter it was a messy opening for my standards the paper was torn completely the president. IT was said that the president was going to visit me tonight. I   know that the president and the 23 were extremely powerful he was more than my job was worth in fact the letter it explained that there had been a new arrival and my job had been done the only thoughts were of my son would I ever see them again.

Eleven thirty I sipped coffee from a mug in the kitchen I was on my own which was not unusual. The next thing which was about to change was the meditation I had lost the power to meditate I had been cut off. I sat down I had not realized at first I crossed over my legs I was already stripped down and I had closed my eyes there was nothing I tried again. And nothing,

"weird" I said to myself.

I tried it on standing up so I did and nothing again. I had one more chance I played down on the floor keeping my cool I closed my eyes it was bang on twelve o'clock the clock in the hall way clock chimed. Again my mind did not move I walked to my bedroom opened the door since I had been meditating I had a voice activated door lock on my bedroom door so nobody would disturb me. I sat on my bed and waited. I was just about to close my eyes when my mind came active again full on. It was Cool It was different. I could feel total peace and my mind was open. I could visualize everything I could see the princess sitting on her throne she spoke out. The term she used was that she was with me, then one of the seven I was told was approaching me I hovered up off the floor the power he welded was incredible he said his words to me where I am your son he put one hand on my shoulder then walk away to join his mother at her side.

Then the Cat turned up.
"Still looking for a body cat"
I called out again.
I have not forgotten what you did Cat.
The cat swiveled and turned around and went and stood beside my son.

I did not smoke often but really fancied a ciggy I put my hands deep into the pocket of my jacket I could feel everything lose change, at the first touch I could feel some money then my second feeling was my lighter, then nothing. I began to pat myself down searching desperately for my cigarettes. Then I remembered that they were down stairs on the bottom of the stairs case inside the pocket of my other jacket. So down stairs I went skipping down the stairs I had found what I was looking for. I had to smile. While I was smoking this fine cigarette. I decided to think about God. It was God that gave me the gift of meditation, then something strange happened I went to put the cigarette out still thinking about God I went back upstairs in to one of my bedrooms and stood looking at my mirror I was posing when I burnt myself with my cigarette it was not so painful at first but then I notice that the flesh under health my skin was white this gave me the conclusion that the whole world was white and color was just another test, this gave me an idea I
had to meditate again I had to find the president and 23

Somehow all this meditation slowly beginning to add up and going back to the very start of my story everything that I learnt. The meeting
of the Cat I hate to mention its name, the president and 23, the tramp, the corpse who is my dead father myself, the Princess, Dave, Eugene were all inter linked. I was coming to the conclusion that it was for the fight for world

spiritual peace. In all of this the only person who I had not seen was the devil and I was not too keen on meeting him and we all know he is about. Maybe he did not have time for me. There were many stories of me members who had lost their minds while traveling around their own body's and their souls were taken and destroyed the princess spoke of this. So it was import ant that I send out the right message after that conversation with my consciousness. I entered the film studios again I was ready to stay the night. I knew of the surrounding straight away and I knew what to expect. A box of chocolate and a bottle of champagne when I got to my chair. It was exactly as it was the first time. The same thoughts were recurring there was nothing out of place. Everything was perfect, I was thinking about the how's and whys and being in the studios made it easier as there was little sound it was peacefully quiet. I was trying to figure out what was the reason for me to be here. I made way towards the chair to sit down but when I did I fell through the chair onto the floor My chair the actors chair was not there it was an illusion. Throwing the devil out had left me quite harmonious and peaceful, I had not said a prey for a while as I was caught in two worlds. Through meditation was a kind of prey. I had not been down on my knees to thank God I was about to do so. My son was growing up fast he was growing up and I was growing younger. This pleased the princess and myself to watch him grow it was

a little miracle he was a miracle it the greatest miracle it was a real gift and should be nurtured and loved to the highest level every single ounce of it should be loved. Children can be funny. A friend of mine once said a child could be more intelligent than its bearers so watch out. But a child will follow to learn, they can be greedy and tormented

, hateful they are pretty good lyres too. But they can be extremely honest and they will always need love I guess everybody does in the end. They can be powerful to that's why we use them on this planet in our world children are sacred. Any way that's enough about that I thought.

My next actions were to get drunk I had not be drunk for quite a while tell a small lie I had a drink last winter when I was on the film set. I walked down stairs to my study I expected to meet Eugene on the way. I stubble as I entered the room I was not drunk yet. I was looking for a bottle of champagne but it was not there right I said to myself I'll have to go down to the wine cellar so I did. There was always a bottle down there, the stairs were steep and the walls were cold to touch. I ran my hand down the wall to the bottom of the banister. I looked around I had a large collection as you already know it did not take me long to find another bottle of bubbly that's when I hesitated I was not sure whether I should take the bottle or not I looked up at the celling and pushed my hand down on the stairs as I climbed to the top. I put the bottle down on my drawing table. I sat down on

my chair taking everything into my mind it felt weird just sitting

chapter38 Outside

there I had not done this for a while It felt quite good to this time I did not close my eyes.

He had made enough money from one card game to go back to work would you believe it Card playing. we spoke he said he had won in the regions of five hundred thousand just in card games and he had a small fortune in a stash you know in case of emergencies of around four million. And how did I know about this well he left his phone on my table. It was one of those cheesy flip top one's kind of funny considering the circumstances. The tight get that explains why he chooses to keep his mouth shut.

I was feeling a light chill I wanted to get a fire started but it was getting a little late I stayed in the chair until the early hours of the morning. Passing in and out of consciousness I did not get really get any sleep. Well as for a glass of champagne there was only so much in the end it was not worth it and I could not be bothered to go all the way down stairs I put the empty bottle down on the table and sat back in the arm chair it was so comfortable and I just sat there taking everything into my mind. It felt quite good just sitting there I had not done this for a while as I was always on the floor or standing up meditation or sitting down.

By the time I had woken up it was twelve o'clock, there was no point in getting up so I waited until about six pm. That's when I got off the sofa. I was feeling a little rough, I clambered into the shower. The water was hot it was soothing to and it felt good to feel the water touch my body. After seven minutes under the shower I grabbed the soap bar and started to wash seven minutes later I climbed out of the shower and began to dry myself on my towel. Now that I was dry I could wax my hair. I always waxed my hair once

162

I was done I went and sat down in my director chair. This was great there was nobody around I noticed a beer in front of me on a small table. There were some flowers on the table I could smell them. The set had changed too. That explained the noise in the middle of the night. This time on the set there was a bed and this was the final scene. I was going to die while making love the scene goes me and this girl in the film have a fling the husband walks in and sees us together then he shoots her she's on top that's great. There was blood everywhere, tomato ketchup.

There were around 53 scenes in this production it was a short film with a big budget, why I was there. I was in the last eight scenes that means there was four scenes to go as I had just finished meditated. The film in its self was good it was getting more and more exciting as each scene passed.
It had been a good and hard year and a half. I had not meditated for a while now, but my other self-kept me in focus,
and told me what was going on with my son. The word was that he was growing up fast and he had already found a plane. I wondered about my other self he always said follow him but when I did he would shy away always trying to hide his face or hide behind objects like tables and chairs and more often the curtains and he was always doing things with his hands like jigsaws or knitting. The other day I saw him knitting a jumper it was for me. But then the thought captured my mind. Who was the real father of this child?
I looked down at cigar that I was smoking it was near its end a couple more puffs, the sensation of the smoke was too strong for me it was quite unbearable but I finished it off with ease. I threw the end of the cigar which was called the butt on to the floor and stamped on it hard into the ground. Then I picked it up off the floor and put it in my pocket.
Back at the mobile unit I had left my music on there was nothing left for me to do. I walked into my dressing room and I fell asleep rather quickly.
The next morning, I awoke early it was the 42dnd scene was at hand I knew it was the forty second scene because I had
read the script fully. By now I had leant my lines it was going to be my turn again soon.
I was a break dancer and people came from all over to watch I was good. The burn is what we called it, I was dressed in a red tracksuit and an old school pair of trainers. The first line was "my father never brought me anything and it was all my mother's money and that was not a lot".
The second line was that "my father was a tight get he keep every penny for

himself". The third line was "I have seen him in the next life. The part went on and on and as I did I got better and better. The lines flowed out of me putting me into a better mood the feeling was incredible. Then nothing, silence. and then an applauded.

With All the promotions there was around twenty million
"that's a hell of a lot of loot, I'm your best friend."
"I know".
"Know I mean it".
"Eugene made five hundred thousand on the cat walk Yesterday she got a check and on top of that she got another three hundred thousand for the movie".
"I on the other hand made seven and a half million on a game of lack jack I bluffed my way right from the stative got his car, house, oil, everything he was some flash dummy from America.
He had a pair of eights I had nothing, he thought I had something and he folded.,"
"Well you look good".
"Okay that's enough about money".
"Well that's all good news what's on the two in the morning, we laughed, cried and eventually went to bed.
The next Morning, I walked into the living room "what's going on here."
"hay "
"hi".
I jumped into the arm chair it was my chair. It was my chair and nobody sat in my chair it was house rules.
And the second was that nobody disturbs me while the footballs on.
    "well" I said, there was a pause "How is everybody".
    "so Dave how did it really go".
    "It went really well how much did you really make?".
    "After tax and Agents fees".
    "obviously"
    "Sorry I cannot tell you it is not that I do not want to tell you it is too hard to account after all the promotions and TV. The film its self-will properly makes a hundred million in the next year".
    I was the lead.

It would have been really good if Eugene could have known my child, Anyway I Had to get home there was something that I had to do I had to spend more time with Dave and Eugene or they would suspect something. So we spent a few more days loving the house which I was trying to sell. My mum came over to she was a funny old lady. All I kept on saying as a joke was how does she like her tea she never caught on. It was Wednesday I told the others that I had had enough over a game of twister you know that old on the floor board game I walked trying to look necked as If I was about to pass out to my bedroom. I thought that they had sassed me out when I was called back but I politely declined. If they found out that all I did was sleep all day I mean how much sleep does the actor need.

I transcended back into the journey it was colorful there was a huge forest that kept on coming into my mind me and the princess had spoken about it. I wanted to be with her all the time I was in love with her just her appearance and she was always polite to her people she was a giver of life like a water fall forever flowing with knowledge she was forgiving we had often spoke about bathing there, there was a river close by.

I had just awoken I was woken by the TV it took me a few seconds to gather my soul and mind I got up and got dressed put on a shirt which I left untucked, a jumper, brief, socks and jeans in that order, I stood by my bedroom window for a minute.

Everybody was in the great hall in the palace that's all I could see it was like being famous twice over once on the earth and the second on the plane. The Cat had the camera and it was taking pitchers of all the people who were dancing, cheering and clapping. You name it, it was a great celebration. There were all kinds of kind people here in the palace. I was about to take my eye off the Cat when I looked up all I could see was the president and 23 stuffing their faces I looked back down The food was of the highest quality although it was very small in stature as you already know. There were children running everywhere in the hall ways and jesters juggling and playing with the fire eaters. It was a modern futuristic palace with a medieval touch added with a little bit of outa space.

On the next day I awoke in her arms half asleep on the dining table I was still in the palace. I had forgot to meditate myself back as I was so drunk from the night before. I had thought of Eugene for the first time in ages I had crated this all of this by chance. It was the first time that I thought of inviting my friends into my world, I was not sure I knew that the princess knew what I was thinking although I wanted more time to think about this there was no way I was going to give them up just yet.

The president was there he said to me look at this letter again please, the message had changed he asked if it was my doing. 23 returned my job to me. It was like I had become extremely powerful and it was said that I was now a teacher and should be   watched over the day and night.

In the next days the Cat had tried to befriend me again for the second time he claimed was just being a Cat and he said that he desperate to get his body back. He was searching for a body like mine. He laughed a lot while we spoke about this it was properly true but I have my doubts that he will find one.

Although I thought that everything was going good all the time my luck was about to change. It started first thing in the next morning I had a letter. The postman came up to the door he
CHAPTER 36 THE CAT

knocked loudly and waited. I was a bit slow to answer the door I had a letter it was marked special delivery. I just caught him as he turned his back.

"Hi there how are you doing "I put my American accent just to impress him.

"your mail". He said.

"Cheers have a nice day". I replied I was in a rush to open it the envelope I mean in it was the letter. I ripped it open I found a letter it was a messy opening for my standards the paper was torn completely the president. It was said that the president was going to visit me tonight. I know that the president and the 23 were extremely powerful he was more than my job was worth in fact the letter it explained that there had been a new arrival and my job had been done the only thoughts were of my son would I ever see them again.

Eleven thirty I sipped coffee from a mug in the kitchen I was on my own which was not unusual. The next thing which was about to change was the meditation I had lost the power to meditate again I had been cut off. I sat down I had not realized at first I crossed over my legs I was already stripped down and I had closed my eyes there was nothing I tried again. And nothing, "weird" I said.

I tried it on standing up so I did and nothing again. I had one more chance I played down on the floor keeping my cool I closed my eyes it was bang on twelve o'clock the clock in the hall way chimed and again and again and again my mind did not move. I walked to my bedroom opened the doors since I had been meditating I had a voice activated door lock on my bedroom door so nobody could disturb me. I sat on my bed and waited. I was just about to close my eyes when my mind came active again full on. It was cool It was different I could feel total peace and my mind was open. I could visualize everything I could see the princess sitting on her throne she spoke out. The term she used was that she was with me, then one of the seven I was told was approaching me I hovered up off the floor the power he welded was incredible he said his words to me where I am your son he put one hand on my shoulder then walk away to join his mother at her side.

Then the Cat turned up.
"Still looking for a body cat"
I called out again.
I have not forgotten what you did Cat.
The cat swiveled and turned around and went and stood beside my son.

I did not smoke often but really fancied a ciggy I put my hands deep into the pocket of my jacket I could feel everything lose change, at first touch I could feel some money then my second feel was my lighter, then nothing. I began to pat myself down searching desperately for my cigarettes Then I remembered that they were down stairs on the bottom of the stair case inside the pocket of my other jacket. So down stairs I went running down the stairs I had found what I was looking for. While I was smoking this fine cigarette. I decided to think about God. It was God that gave me the gift of meditation, then something strange happened I went to put the cigarette out still thinking about God I went back upstairs in to one of my bedrooms and stood looking at a wall mirror I was posing when I burnt myself with my cigarette it was not so painful at first but then I notice that the flesh under health my skin was white this gave me the conclusion that the whole world was white and color was just another test, this gave me an idea I

had to meditate again I had to find the president and 23 me ask them about what I had stubble upon and if they agreed.

Somehow all this meditation and going back to the very start of my story everything that I learnt. The meeting

of the Cat I hate to mention its name, the president and 23, the tramp, the corpse who is my dead self, the princess, Dave, Eugene and myself were all inter linked. I was coming to the conclusion that it was for the fight for world spiritual peace. In all of this the only person who I had not seen was the devil and I was not too keen on meeting him and we all know he is about. Maybe he did not have time for. There were many stories of me members who had lost their minds while traveling around their own body's and their souls were taken and destroyed. So it was import ant that I send out the right message with after that conversation with my consciousness throwing the devil out had left me quite harmonious and peaceful, I had not said a prey for a while as I was caught in two worlds. Through meditation was a kind of prey. I had not been down on my knees to thank God I was about to do so. My son was growing up fast he was growing up and I was growing younger. This pleased the princess and myself to watch him grow it was

a little miracle he was a miracle it the greatest miracle it was a real gift and should be nurtured and loved to the highest level every single ounce of it should be loved. Children can be funny. A friend of mine once said a child could be more intelligent than its bearers so watch out. But a child will follow to learn, they can be greedy and tormented

, hateful they are pretty good lyres too. But they can be extremely honest and they will always need love I guess everybody does in the end. They can be powerful to that's why we use them on this planet in our world children are sacred. Any way that's enough about that I thought.

My next actions were to get drunk I had not be drunk for quite a while tell a small lie had a drink last winter I was on the film set. I walked down stairs to my study I expected to meet Eugene on the way. I stubble as I entered the room was not yet drunk I was looking for a bottle of champagne but it was not there right I said to myself I'll have to go down to the wine cellar so I did. There was always a bottle down there, the stairs were steep and the walls were cold to touch. I ran my hand down the wall to the bottom of the banister. I looked around I had a large collection as you already know it did not take me long to find another bottle of bubbly that's when I hesitated I was not sure whether I should take the bottle or not I looked up at the celling and pushed my hand on the down onto the stairs. I put the bottle down on my drawing table in my study. I sat down on my chair taking everything into my mind it felt weird just sitting there I had not done this for a while It felt quite good this time I closed my eyes.

he had made enough money from one card games to go back to work would you believe it card playing. We spoke he said he had won in the regions of five hundred thousand just in card games and he had a small fortune in there you know in case of emergencies of around four million. And how did I know about this well he left his phone on my table. It was one of those cheesy flip top one's kind of funny considering the circumstances. The tight get.

I was feeling a light chill I wanted to get a fire started but it was getting a little late I stayed in the chair until the early hours of the morning. Passing in and out of consciousness I did not get really get any sleep. Well as for a glass of champagne there was only so in the end it was not worth it and I could not be bothered to go all the way down stairs I put the bottle down on the table and sat back in the arm chair it was so comfortable and I just sat there taking everything into my mind. It felt quite good just sitting there I had not done this for a while as I was always on the floor or standing up meditation or sitting down.

By the time I had woken up it was twelve o'clock, there was no point in getting up so I waited until about six pm. That's when I got off the sofa. I was feeling a little rough, I clambered into the shower. The water was hot it was soothing to and it felt good to feel the water touch my body. After seven minutes under the shower I grabbed the soap bar and started to wash seven minutes later I climbed out of the shower and began to dry myself on my towel. Now that I was dry I could wax my hair. I always waxed my hair once that was done I went and sat down in my director's chair. This was great there was nobody around I noticed a beer in front of me on a small table. There were some flowers on the table I could smell them. The set had changed too. That explained the noise in the middle of the night. This time on the set there was a bed and this was the final scene. I was going to die while making love the scene goes me and this girl in the film have a fling the husband walks in and s eyes us together then he shoots her she son top that's great. There was blood everywhere. tomato ketchup.

to it. There were around 53 scenes in this production it was a short film with a big budget, why I was there. I was in the last eight scenes that means there was four scenes to go as I had just fin meditated fished four. The film in its self was good it was getting more and more exciting as each scene passed.

It had been a good and hard year and a half. I had not meditated for a while now, but my other self-kept me in focus,

and told me what was going on with my son. The word was that he was growing up fast and he had already found a plane. I wondered about my other self he always said follow him but when I did he would shy away always trying to hide his face or hide behind objects like tables and chairs and more often the curtains and he was always doing things with his hands like jigsaws or knitting. The other day I saw him knitting a jumper it was for my child. But then the thought captured my mind. Who was the real father of this child?

I looked down at cigar that I was smoking it was near its end a couple more puffs, the sensation of the smoke was too strong for me it was quite unbearable but I finished it off with ease. I threw the end of the cigar which was called the butt on to the floor and stamped on it hard into the ground. Then I picked it up off the floor and put it in my pocket.

Back at the mobile unit I had left my music oh overpromise there was nothing left for me to do. I fell asleep rather quickly.

The next morning, I awoke early it was the 42dnd scene was at hand I knew it was the forty second scene because I had

read the script fully. By now I had leant my lines it was going to be my turn again soon.

I was a break dancer and people came from all over to watch I was good. The burn is what we called it, I was dressed in a red tracksuit and an old school pair of trainers. The first line was "my father never brought me anything and it was all my mother's money and that was not a lot".

The second line was that "my father was a tight get he keep every penny for himself". the third line was "I have seen him in the next life and his poor, it did sadden me a lot.

I pulled the cigarette out of my shirt pocket and put one in my mouth. This is where I get frustrated I've lost my lighter again not to worry I do not get worried about things like that. I had a backup plan. I went into the studios kitchen, I thought it would be a good idea to light it off one of the cookers. It could work so I did two minutes later I found my lighter. Better luck next time I guess. I took a deep breath and a puff of the fag the taste was strong I mean really strong. I went back to my accommodation when I got into the van I was looking at a picture of my dad

"so dad ". I said to the picture "how poor are we".
There was now answer "oh the strong silence type".
I said it again holding the picture down only expecting that in some way some kind of immaculate conception would speak but nothing. That's when I realized that he was really gone. Somehow just touching the picture brought all the emotions back. My eyes filled up with tears but I fought it and fought it well. I was not going to waste my tears on him. I turned the picture over then I hesitated and turned the picture back over then I told it that I had no time for tears and I was sorry. I turned the Music on lent back in my chair and took my mind off it.

I knew something was missing I loved listening to music I always thought that I would be a dancer of some sort but that's a whole different story.

It begins way in the eighties I had put the money ventures down and turned to hip hop.

I took my hand off and pushed the open the door just next door was a couple of drunk actors they were stubbing outside their van. I could not see who it was but it sounded like the other two lead actors who have main parts with me.

They were definitely having fun. All I could hear was laughter. I looked away in shame and shyness then went back inside I took my cap and jacket off and just looked at the table on the table was a pad some pens a candle stick holder some snacks and a drug prescription a bowl and to remote control. It was not easy working on a film set this big you had to know where everything is although I was well catered for also on the table was a picture of my dad he was a royal engineer when he was alive he was a solider I did not really like him I suppose that amounts for something as he spent most of the time beating up my mother and spending most of his life in pub.

Well now I am all grown up and the silly money adventures have become serious make or break discussions everything was going great anyway and I think on the money kind of things I am now even more comfortable it may seem. I got up and laid back father onto the sofa. I was tired and just wanted to go to sleep but I knew that something would disturb my cheeks, more visions and dream, the dreams I could not stand. I walked up to the door in the bedroom the air was hot and the beer that I had been drinking had become stale there was a sign on the door with my name on it. I tried to smudge it off with my fingers then my hand my name I thought on pluck I thought that it was great but annoying

So I had just finished another film it went really well but there's more to come promotions and advertisements.

advertisements, sponsorship, I should make a clear two million then there's fees it's great. I have always liked money. Being Part of the film industry I don't often tell people about the shares I own as I also own the biggest TV company in the world and I also own a film studio amongst other things you are properly wondering how I made so much money. Well it started on guy's folk's night I had nothing to do so I made a guy it was made of old newspapers I played it down on the street between a pub and a corner shop. That was the start of my money making adventure. After this I became a carol singer as I recall it was Christmas I knocked on every house in the village that I was brought up in, it was on a council estate which me and my two brother were housed upon. I sang my nuts off for a whole week during the Christmas holidays and the reward for that was a large bag of money. After this it was down to the spoilers on the barracks where I lived I would wait until they passed me and then I would just stop to speak to them and during the conversation I would ask them for some money. I made enough money on that day to buy myself some sweets. This went on for about a year or so.

But my most favorite adventure was to selling holly. There was a holly tree in the park it took all evening cutting holly from its bush bagging it and selling it. That was good all of my little money making ideas and I have not been able to stop making money today. I do not spend out on everything sometimes I choose to go without things such as tooth paste, clothes, but in saying that the cars are in the garage but I have no silence.

It was night the sky was clear and the stars were out. I opened the front and back doors to let the light fresh air in. I looked around I was amazed just being here on the earth it was a real frill. I could not think of a better place to be, there was a bench in the garden so I walked over to it I sat down un did the buckles on my shoes and closed my eyes and praised the night I was there for a few hours I slowly fell asleep. When I awoke it was early morning there was due on the grass the sun was out I could clearly see it I was sweating I rubbed the sweat off my fore head and then wiped it off onto my knee. I then became extremely wide eyes and awake. I looked up to the clouds they were moving slowly and I watched the moon slowly recede back into space as the sun came out over powering the moon. The love that I could feel from the planet was incredible from the smallest thing to the largest plants they can love to it was like a dream. I came to the conclusion that I had everything the only thing left was for me to drive my car. I jumped up quickly and walked to my garage I already had the keys for my car on me.

As soon as I got back I took off my racing cap and threw it on the side as I walked into the house I had made quite a substantial amount of money I was thinking about selling the mansion for even more money. After everything that I gone through while being here I wondered if it would be worth it. I was still in love with the place. Although My place was good but old and dingy I was looking for something a little bit more modern.

I started to think about the idea of moving more and more. I had to tell the others to see what they would think and say of course I would take them with me. I always had a second opinion which I will be seeking in the near future. Even though it was early morning I decided to sleep through to The next day I woke up early in the morning it was hard trying to find enough sleep when you have so many demons. I slowly got up out of my bed and walked to my wardrobe I picked a shirt out and grabbed the first pair of jeans I could find. Socks, shoes, pants and vest

I went to the window while addressing that winter could be here soon I thought. I looked around the room I was looking for my sweets I had found them they had fallen behind the side cabinet. I had no idea how long they had been there but I needed to. I just wanted something to suck.

Eugene had awoken she explained to me that she had a really tough night she said in our conversation she said she had dreams of golden fields, I held here in my arms. While she tied back her blonde hair. She had a lot for a young person I was around ten years older than her. I stood her up on to her feet she was all floppy I looked at her face

face it she was like she was in a dream tears started pouring down her face they came down two by two both sides I said to her that I could not remember how many times that I had said this to her but you must know by now that we love you and I think that you are a little bit over worked. That's when the expression on her face changed I looked at her hard and gave her a kiss on her fore head. The crying did not stop there the more I tried to calm her the worst she got. I think she was in love.

Winter just around the corner I could feel the change in the air the wind had got colder and on some trees the leaves had fallen. Something was about change I did not know if it was me or the meditation. When I closed my eyes I could not see the planes that I would normally find I could not see the visions the light had become darkness. There was some new people who were entering my mind whatever it was not the rich presents anymore of a clean mind. My thoughts were racing instead of being calm these new people were dangerous. while I was getting a message from the others that were there. I meditated with the cat and the president. I was also being told to

leave the plane to get outside to go anywhere but not into my own mind I was worried for my wife and son how would I see them. There were messages sent to me from a few people the cat and the president again but nothing from my son or my wife. I began to realize that I had stubble upon pure evil it was not death or Satan it was nothing. I wanted to take my mind off things so I decided to do some reading I walked to my study. On the book self was books, comic books laden from top to bottom, such story's as back2back, the Hitman, Master criminal, many many other I had in the region of about two thousand. It took me around fifteen to twenty minutes to find a good comic. I found what I was looking for Spirits memory check, I dipped my hand into the shelf and pulled a couple of books. I jumped down off the ladder and into my chair and opened the first book and began to read it. The comic book script was put together quite well it read cross ways, it had bright colors and the characters were red hot the story line too but that was normal. Boy meets girl, girl gets kidnapped, boy goes after girl and so on. It's the kind of thing I could read for hours I got so engrossed I forgot about the football this evening. The good thing about comic books is that they are never ending they can go on and on and on the way the characters change from time to time the story takes you on a terrible journey they are almost as good as a film script. I enjoy looking at the backs of the book there's always a picture of a super hero on them or the baddies as I call them. Every comic book I brought I actually read. As I recall this was the sixth time I had read this particular book and I still get excited.

What I also like about comic books is the little logo on the top left hand side, you always look at it for a minute before you open it. It is funny it was really quiet a good feeling, it was definitely a good wat to spend your time taking the hustle and the bustle of the world off your shoulders. In one story which was a tear jerker the main character dies. It kind of kills the rest of the story in the comic book.

I put the comic down that I was reading and picked up another. Now this looked good all the colors nice and bright but it was not unusual for comics to be brightly colored. I also like the characters in comic they sound all sound futuristic and not just this they have special super powers I would love to make a movie like this but I know and I see that it has already been done. I could imagine all my super heroes in a film it sounds good to me. Just think special effects, it would cost me a fortune and properly make me another one too.

Something extremely funny was about to happen as I lay there in my bed a robbery was at hand. That's right my beautiful home was about to be burgled. The whole place was belled up, but something went wrong with my alarm systems. There were rumors that there was a thief in the neighborhood it was all over TV and in the local papers. So I guess that why I keep on seeing police cars passing by my mansion, I shall continue it had just gone three o'clock in the morning, when I thought I heard somebody pass my bedroom door. This did not happen once but twice. I had to go and investigate it I picked up my tennis racket which was by the door gripping it tightly and opened the bedroom door gripping the bat even harder that's when I heard the footsteps, I knew it was an intruder because Eugene would have turned on the lights so would have Dave. That's when I heard the burglar's footsteps he was just going to leave. I ran down the corridor dropping the bat not realizing it's the adrenaline pumped through my body hands and arms in racing motion it was just as good as being in the movies.

The adrenaline was pumping reaching out as I was spiriting around the corner into the main corridor and grabbing the thief who was now the victim. With both hands
As this happened Dave was just walking in too.
I've got him
What, what s all the noise
don't move I said as I put the burglar in a head lock on the floor
Dave turn on the lights I shouted
"what"
just do it let un mask this bandit
I could not believe it I pulled off the mask and to my surprise
"Darrell".
"who, who it's you".
"it is being it's you".
"I do not believe it."
"it's me ".
"it's you".
"I have not seen you for years are you still playing football".
" what the hell do you think you were doing".
"what me nothing".
"it does not look like nothing to me ".
Myself and Darrell had already been acquainted we played football together for a couple of years at the local sports center way back in the day."
"I'll take those".
Dave grabbed the sack
"Dave hold on what's in the sack".
"My Rembrandt and oh my Mona".
"flip that's what it's called".
"and my Picasso".
"well what can I say I had fallen on hard times".
"I'd say Dave said joking".
"The kids had grown up the wife has left me I did not have much choice, but you're doing alright though".
I interrupted him quickly.
"Would you like a beer".
"Go on then".
We walked to the kitchen I opened the fridge door and took three beers out.

Dave here's your beer, Darrell and here's yours.

We began talking by the time we had finished it was late morning. I began so you are skin and you need some cash, let me help you Dave can you go to my study and get my cheese book. Darrell's eyes opened wide he knew he was on to something good.

He will not be a minute.

Fifty grand enough.

His eyes widened more.

Yes, yes thank you he said smiling.

But before I give you this you have to solely swear never to burgle again. Oh right all right.

I could tell he was lying. Is that enough I handed him the calque.

That's more than enough he said snatching the money.

Thank you thank you mate. We sat there in the kitchen for a couple more hours after a hand full of beers and an

and an egg and bacon fry up I showed him the door.

I sparked up a cigarette a list of names flooded my head.

I had grown tired of all the meditation and I had also full filled my souls wishes. Everything was going well. The princess had a knew child who I dearly missed but I was very pleased. I was over the moon with my wife and her decisions and the things which had happened between me and her. For some reason I had no recollection of ever having sex with her which was a shame as I always thought about the intermesh of it.

But indeed all the signs were there when we met. I was at home but I had planned to make another visit to my new family. I was in the kitchen when I began to start thinking of everything that had happened there was a reason for everything. The thoughts were racing through my mind. Everything I thought was great but I was wrong. Something terrible was about to happen. I could hear screams coming from the other room. I sprinted across the kitchen down the corridor and into the lower bedroom what I could see was the cat it had attacked Eugene I could see this but Eugene could not.

She screamed out swinging at the air.

What the hell. She screamed

get out I shouted.

And what the hell are you doing in my bed room

pasty bloody creature she cried out.

I got close enough to thump it. But the cat was persistent.

He leaped of the bed and gave a grunt. Want some more do you. It screamed.
What is the problem cat? I shouted.
Who did you just speak to and who's the cat. Eugene asked.
I had to lie, diving on to the floor after the animal I was speaking to you cat
is me knew nickname for you.

I tried shoving her through the bedroom door but she was persistent in
wanting to walk back in this happened three times until I raised my voice
would you please get out of this room?
I walked calmly to the window and opened it. Then I grabbed the pillow
from my bed and unfolded it from its case. I waved it around the bedroom
and tried to disguise the fact that we were being visited.
Eugene sued it straight away.
You can see something what what is it?
Before I had a chance to think of an answer Eugene said to me not to lie to
her.
Nothing I can see nothing.
It was written all over my face. The cat I was told through my mind was
trying to invite Eugene to visit them and to meditate with him.
I could read the cats mind like that.
It's no longer your secret the cat said pausing. We went for each other.
The cat laughed
Ha you missed.
What the hell what was that. Eugene cried out.
What was what. The cat was slowly dismantling my bedroom by throwing
thinks at me and Eugene.
Then I got him.
Got you. I shouted.
The cat was now in the pillow case I rubbed the sweat from my forehead
again and again and threw him out of the window and locked the window
shut.
Eugene watched in amazement although there was nothing to see by her
human eye
yet.
The cat strolled off as usual. I was going to be questioned I just knew it.
What the hell was that. Eugene said.
What was what.

That thing was it a ghost wait ok stop screwing with me.

I know something I mean that was something I said under my breath.

, okay.

That was …. there was a long pause

go on spill it I want the truth. Eugene said.

To be honest I cannot explain right now.

Tell me she said corruptible and quickly with a shock in her voice.

I gulped and she gulped I went to leave the room but Eugene blocked the way by standing in the way of the door.

Tell me tell me please. She went on Is it a secret.

I cannot explain. I raised my voice. Now kindly step out of my way.

No. she stood there firmly in the door way in front of me.

Move I request it. I replied.

Not until you tell me what is going on.

I move closer to her suddenly the clouds in the sky started to move quickly day became night there was another storm brewing. The clouds were moving at a rapid speed's something was wrong I could feel it. A storm had started. Suddenly there was a large bang lightning and thunder. It would have made your knees bend. One minute there was light the next minute total chaos in the sky and darkness.

The wind picked up fast, then it began to rain. Eugene was not thinking she went over to the window leaving the door unmanned then there was a large bang the thunder and lightning had hit the roof the electricity blew we were both in total darkness I managed to slip out of the room in to the darkened corridor.

That damn cat what was he trying to do. I said to myself.

I was not by the sea but it was early morning and I could see sea gulls they could talk a lot like cats but what they were talking about could open a massive scientific conversation. I was always thought that they were playing in some form or another. These particular gulls could speak human too just like cats.

I looked out the window I was upstairs in the spare room the main road a few houses were all I could see not much for a mute -million-pound estate bright lights shining down in a watery reflection of the road caught my eyes. I closed one eye and a tear fell from my face I was not upset a such it seemed or as it seemed I was a little upset about the cat I guess. Somehow I will have

to explain to the others, going back to the birds they for some reason
they reminded me of bats I had not seen a bat for years maybe they had all died or something. I know they exist. Just before I had left the room upstairs I looked in the mirror I had grown even younger it was stupid and though it gave me a scare. I was glad I was the only person who could see this. But the pain did not leave it got worse and worse I looked down at my hands as I ran cold water on them it was soothing at the bedroom sink.

The swelling was immense they were feeling quite painful I started to cry tears ran down my face I needed to pull myself together I needed to meditate as I went to turn around I knocked a glass off the sinks side top it had smashed on the floor I quickly tidied it up I went down stairs and went to go into my room. The pain became so hard I passed out for a minute or two I was thinking about the cat. I sensed that something was wrong I got off my bed and sat in my chair crossed my legs and closed my eyes then that's when it happened the cat had got its claws out it was in my mind it jumped on me scratching my face and yelling at me I grappled with it pushing it onto the floor, my first instincts was to kick it but for some reason I went to pick up a pillow instead. It leaped at me, I took a swipe with the pillow, I missed just.
Bloody hell, I said out loud.

The cat attack was nearly over I did not know why he was attacking me I did not know what I had done there was a short pause which gave me time to take the pillow out of its case I could use the case as a weapon.

Right you little get. I shouted as I raced towards it as it raced towards me it was going for my jugular I was told this time he missed stretching my arm.

You little bastard I shouted as I positioned myself for the next attack. It came at me again this time I swing a right hook and caught him in the jaw and winded it

my arm was stretched up bad by this time I took the pillow case again and dived at it across the room but I missed. It ran across the room and leaped out of the window into my garden I ran up to the window and closed it tightly.

What the hell I thought that cat is turning into a real handful I tidied the room up quickly luckily I did not make too much mess as before or too much noise. I opened and closed the window to make sure that the window was closed properly.

It was time for a change, there was many things which I had to take in to consideration stupid things, silly things such as what I was having for breakfast what I wearing, simple things like what aftershave I was using how many times away I would brush my teeth. I was also beginning to realize that my actions and the things I did had consequences and affected other people. I could hear the sound of seagulls in the sky it was funny. It reminded me of the conversation we had last time I met the bird. It was late there was a knock on the door I knew who it was it was Dave my cop. I greeted him with a smile he gave me a hand shake and a kiss and a hug. He was not surprised when I asked him where Eugene was he said properly at the club. He was wrong.

He struggled his shoulders and said leave me alone. He was drunk. What happened next was extremely saddening it broke my heart it was the cat a complained by the tramp who gave me the message the king whom we all dearly loved had other plans for my princess. She was told never to contact me again. She had been told that we cannot meditate again and she was told that she must avoid all humans from now on. And our child was never to be mentioned on a human planet or plane again. Whatever happens now was going to be very costly. The cat and the tramp left my side. For some reason the cat had a big grin on its face I asked it why are you smiling in reply to this he just said nothing he just stared at me. That's when I clicked okay what have you done. The cat reply to this was to blow on his right paw then he rubbed his chest and said.

No shit.

He then continued.

She's next door if you want her she's quite weak at the moment she will properly never come back.

I leaped on to my feet and stood watching the cat and the tramp walk off into the distance. Dam I never knew I walked quickly to Eugene's bedroom there I heard a voice the voice said in a kind of whisper I must not disturb her but I ignored it. And knelt down by her bedroom door looking through the key hole. Eugene was sitting crossed legged on her bed. There was nothing I could do.

THE END